SHARON A. MITCHELL

REASONS

BOOKS

By Sharon A. Mitchell

When Bad Things Happen

GONE

TRUST

SELFISH

INSTINCT

REASONS WHY

MINE

SANCTUM

Vinci Books

vinci-books.com

Published by Vinci Books Ltd in 2025

1

A CIP catalogue record for this book is available from the British Library.
Paperback ISBN: 9781036707545

The EU GPSR authorised representative is Logos Europe, 9 rue Nicolas Poussion, 17000 La Rochelle, France
contact@logoseurope.eu

Part I

Chapter One

It hadn't been bad while the sun was up, but now that darkness filled the car, it was damp and chilly. All three girls huddled in the back seat, using each other's bodies for warmth. Twelve-year-old Sally was in the middle, an arm around each of her sisters.

The streetlight across the road shone a beam into the dusty car's interior. Sally saw that Bethany's eyes were closed, her head slumped onto her chest. That kid could sleep anywhere. But she couldn't be comfortable like that. Gently, Sally eased the five-year-old down into a prone position, her head on Sally's thighs, her legs stretched across Laura's.

They waited. And waited some more.

"Geez, how long is Mom going to be?"

It had been several hours already. Mom said she was stopping in for a quick drink and a bite to eat with her friends.

"I'm thirsty." Laura was only voicing what played on Sally's mind, too.

Sally was thankful that they had no drinks in the car. If they'd guzzled pop or water, especially Bethany, who knew how many times she'd have needed to pee? As far as Sally could see, there was no store around where they could ask to use a washroom.

Although her eyes remained closed, Bethany stirred restlessly in her sleep. She brought her knees to her chest, inadvertently kicking Laura in the stomach.

"Get her off me! She kicked me! Little twerp. Thinks she can pretend to be asleep and get away with kneeing me."

"She *is* asleep. She didn't mean it." Sally looked at her little sister's soft face. Instead of her usual placid sleeping expression, there was a slight frown. Her hands were under her armpits, a move Sally had taught her to warm herself up. There was a slight vibration. There it was again, more regular now. The child was shivering. Quickly, trying not to wake the child, Sally stripped off her own coat and draped it over the sleeping little girl. Soon, the shivering stopped, and Bethany's face took on the relaxed repose only small children achieve.

Laura shuffled closer, her arm and side plastered to Sally's. She tucked her hands alongside Bethany's legs, underneath Sally's jacket. Although only ten, Laura's instincts for self-preservation were well honed.

Getting chillier by the second, Sally's hands joined her sisters' under the jacket, tucking them into the space where Bethany's upper arms met her shoulders. That warmed her hands a bit, but did little for the rest of her.

"Sally, you have to do something. We can't stay here all night."

True. This had happened to them before, but when the temperatures were warmer. Now it had to be in the low 50s

- not bad when you're walking around and dressed for it, but definitely uncomfortable for three girls huddled in the back seat of an old car.

Periodically the door of the bar opened, letting out a rectangle of light, raucous laughter and the stench of stale, spilled beer. As the door let out another burst of forced hilarity, the girls instinctively ducked. This was not their first rodeo. Mom gave strict orders to stay out of sight and silent so no one would know they were there. They'd had experiences before of strange men trying to get into the car with them. Even though she had checked, rechecked and checked yet again, Sally glanced at the door locks to make sure they were fastened. Sally appreciated that their mother had taken care to park the car away from any direct pool of light that illuminated the contents of the car.

The shaking started again, this time not from the smallest sister, but from Sally.

"Keep still," Laura complained. "You are so annoying."

"I'm shivering. I can't help it."

"Well, you're the dummy who took off her coat."

Sally glanced at the features of her sister that were visible in the murky light. How could Laura be so self-centered? Sally was positive that at ten, she'd had more consideration for others than Laura showed.

"I gotta pee." This from Laura, again.

"You'll have to hold it. I don't see any place around here with a washroom."

"If I pee my pants, you'll be sorry."

True, thought Sally. All of us will be sorry and the car would stink for weeks. It had happened before.

"When did Mom say she was coming back?"

"She didn't, just that she wouldn't be long."

"But this is long, isn't it?"

5

To Sally, it sure seemed it. Neither of them had a watch, but it had been dark for almost two hours now. It felt like at least nine o'clock, but who knew.

"I'm hungry." Laura, Miss Obvious.

"Who isn't?"

"I bet he isn't." Laura pointed to the older man leaving the bar on wobbly legs. He rested one hand along the brick exterior of the building to get his balance, before shaking his head and making a serpentine line for the car two spaces ahead of them. After a lengthy period of fumbling, he managed to get the car door open and pour himself behind the driver's seat. He sat there with his head back for a while, the door still ajar.

"What's he doing?" Laura asked.

"I dunno. Resting, maybe?"

"He just came from the bar. Mom says the place relaxes her. How can he need to rest if he's just been in a relaxing place?

Sally had no answer.

Bethany made little noises with her mouth as she exhaled in her sleep. Sally wasn't positive, because the windows were down, but she thought the man made *big* noises from his mouth as he caught some zzz's behind the wheel of his car. With a snort and a gasp audible two cars away, the man came to. Seconds later, there was the sound of his engine starting. Then his car swung away from the curb, veered to the far side of the street, then righted itself into the correct lane, and was gone.

At least that broke their boredom for a few minutes, but now that that distraction was gone, Sally's brain reminded her once again of the distress her body was in. Her shivering was non-stop now, and intensifying. If she couldn't get it under control, she'd wake Bethany. A rudely woken

Bethany was a cranky Bethany; no one wanted that, especially when they were confined to the interior of an old car.

Sally needed to do something. Trying to do a brain meld with their mom was not working, at least not so far, and she'd really tried.

The orders were to not leave the car. But what if the three of them turned into icicles before their mom returned? What if she forgot about them? What if she went home with someone else? She didn't always come home from the bar, especially after meeting some friends she wanted to get closer to.

As gently as she could, Sally eased her legs out from under Bethany's head and shoulders. She made herself as skinny as she could in the small space between the little girl's dark curls and the door. "Here, you move over and let her use your legs for a pillow," she told Laura.

About to refuse out of sheer habit, Laura realized that it might be a warmer position. She wormed her way under Bethany's body without disturbing the child's slumber. She, too, did not want to wake up Bethany. "What are you going to do?"

"I'm going to see if I can find Mom."

"About time." Laura leaned her head back against the stained seat and closed her eyes.

The door was heavy and required wrapping both of her hands around the vertical bar and heaving. Maybe it would have been easier on another day, but Sally's hands were partially numb from the cold and she hadn't eaten since breakfast.

Once inside, Sally froze to the spot. Then, she moved

into the shadows at the side to scout the place. There were lights, but not nearly enough to see clearly. There was noise, all kinds of noise, especially that funny kind of barking laugh people gave when they'd been drinking. Or, at least her mom did and the gentlemen friends she brought home.

Although some establishments employed a ban on smoking indoors, this one obviously didn't. Or, if it did, no one heeded the rules. The wafting layers of smoke made it hard to make out individual patrons seated around the tables.

It would help if Sally knew the friends her mom was with, but Mom's friends changed rapidly, depending on her mood, she said. So, Sally had no idea who her mom was relaxing with.

Relaxing? This was not Sally's idea of relaxing. Relaxing was that odd moment when she could sneak off the library alone, when she could browse the stacks, working her way through the Dewey Decimal system, filling her mind with whatever facts she wanted to study at the time. Relaxing was those rare moments when she and Mom would sit out on the back stoop, just the two of them and talk, really talk. Or, Mom would talk and Sally would listen; it was a way to get to know the different sides to the woman who had given her life.

But this place? The wavering lights filtering through the smoke. The incessant noise of laughing, boasting, and people talking over one another, vying for attention. The clink of the billiard balls in the corner. The ball game on the big screen TV in the corner by the bar. The country music blasting in the other corner. Relaxing? Her thumb rubbed against the side of her index finger, over and over and over again.

There were so many angles to this room, so many people who didn't stay still. Realizing she'd never find her mother from this vantage point, Sally moved farther into the room, each footstep sticking slightly to the floor. It was like that time Laura spilled strawberry jam on the floor, but only wiped up the most obvious part of the red goo, thinking herself hard done by to have had to do that much. For days their socks would stick to the floor before Sally washed away all traces of the accident. Perhaps she could get a job here washing the floor. She'd need a mask, though, or some kind of breathing filter to hide the stench of old beer.

What did people here have against lights? Sally had priced them in the store - 100-watt bulbs costs the same amount as 40-watt ones. So, why not shine a little light in this place?

There! It didn't peal out often at home, but when her mom laughed, no one could help but join in. Freezing to the spot, Sally moved only her head, focusing her hearing on that particular sound. There! Her mom's laugh, followed by a bunch of deeper, louder guffaws.

"Hey! You don't look twenty-one."

A man set down the glass he was filling and came from behind the bar, wiping his hands on the stained white apron stretched over his girth. His pace quickened as he got closer to Sally, hands on hips, looming over her. Sally had seen friendlier visages from Laura when she was told she couldn't have something she wanted.

Taking a step backwards, Sally's foot slid in a puddle. Her efforts to balance herself splashed the liquid onto the hem of her jeans.

"Well, little girl? What are you doing in here? Trying to get me shut down?" He pointed to the door with the blinking, red and white exit sign over it. "Out! Git out of here, now!"

"Please sir, I'm trying to find my mom. I just need to speak to her, then I'll go. Promise."

Izzy's laugh rang out again, flying overtop the cacophony of sounds reverberating through this room. Before the man could grab her arm and throw her out, Sally ducked and pivoted, homing in on the sound.

There. At that crowded table. No wonder she hadn't seen Mom when she came in. Izzy was surrounded by people. Of course. Both men and women pointed their faces in Izzy's direction, hanging onto her words. Oh, this was mom at her best, eyes flashing, visage animated, in control and relishing the spotlight.

Sally stood at the edge of the group, peeking between heads. Even though the men were sitting, some of them still towered over Sally. Behind her, she heard the heavy stomp of the barkeeper coming up behind her. She didn't have much time. "Mom!" She tried for both volume and authority in her voice at the same time. "Mom!"

The gentleman in the chair closest to Sally turned his head. "Whoa, a kid. What's a kid doing in here?" He moved his chair back half a foot, as if she had cooties and he didn't want to catch them.

His chair banged that of the man next to him. That, and his words snagged the attention of his nearest neighbors. In a matter of seconds, all conversation around the crowded table stopped and all eyes turned to Sally.

Izzy's exuberant face turned Sally's way. Like a deflating balloon, all the animation drained away. She said not a word.

"Mom?"

The barkeeper was behind Sally now. His beefy hand

came down hard on her shoulder. "Does someone belong to this kid?"

No one spoke.

His grip tightened.

Izzy's eyes remained on the table where she swirled a sweaty bottle of beer and set it in its damp ring on the table.

More quieter now, "Mom?"

In the rest of the room, speech and laughter and braggart stories gradually died down as if some unspoken message had spread that there was drama about. All eyes turned Sally's way, that is, all eyes, but for Izzy's.

"Mom, we need to go. Bethany's been asleep for hours. We're cold. And Laura has to pee."

That brought a roar of laughter from the crowd. Finally, Izzy's gaze met that of her daughter's.

Oh, no. Sally knew that unfocused look, as if her mom was not quite in control of her vision. The rest of her body wouldn't be much more coordinated, either. Sally squared her shoulders. It was okay. They'd dealt with this before. She gave a brief thought for how they were going to get their mother up the three flights of stairs to their apartment, while carrying a sleeping Bethany. But, she'd worry about that later. For now, she had to get her mom out to the car.

"Lady," the voice boomed from above Sally's head. "We don't allow no kids in this place. She doesn't even *look* twenty-one. You're gonna get me shut down. Take your kid and get out of here." When Sally didn't move, he released his hand from its grip on Sally's shoulder and took a step towards Izzy. There was a shuffling of chairs as both men and women tried to make way in the crowded space.

Sally smelled his body odor as he brushed by her. "Mom, come on." Izzy didn't move. What would this guy do to her if she didn't? His face was not friendly. Nor did he have what Sally called a leer, but mom called it bedroom eyes. Instead, his look was plain nasty. Living where they did, Sally had learned to avoid those types.

"Mom." Sally tried to use the tone she employed when trying to make Laura do something she didn't want to do. "We have to go *now*! The kids can't wait any longer."

"Wait." The hand on her shoulder spun Sally around. "Do you mean to tell me that you kids have been waiting in the car whole time your mom's been in here?"

Sally didn't mean to tell him anything. She just wanted to get her mom and leave. But his eyes left her no choice. They clearly stated that she was not moving an inch until she answered his question. So, she nodded.

The man narrowed his eyes at her, but his grip on her shoulder loosened. Instead, he turned that ugly look onto Izzy.

Uh oh. Now Sally'd be in for it if she got her mom into trouble. "Please, mister. It's all right, but we need to go now."

He gave a quick glance at Sally, then returned his glare to Izzy's wobbling head. "Are you trying to ruin my business? You can get me shut down for having an underage kid in here." His chin pointed at Sally. "Second, the cops don't look well on me having patrons who dump their kids in the car outside while they get sloshed in here."

"I'm not sloshed," insisted Izzy. But there was an extra "SH"at the beginning of the word. She heard it herself, and tried to correct it. "Shoshed. No, shloshed." She tried again. "I'm not drunk." There. She nodded, pleased with herself for getting it right.

The barkeeper approached Izzy's chair. Men quickly shoved their chairs out of the way, giving the looming giant easier access to Izzy. Not one of them attempted to interfere with the beefy hand that wrapped around Izzy's upper arm. Giving a tug, he joisted Izzy out of her seat.

In her semi-boneless state, she came up easily, listing to the side, and would have face-planted, if not for his hold on her arm. "Get your hands off me!"

Almost in unison, came "Get your hands off my mother!"

Izzy's and Sally's eyes met. A slow smile spread across Izzy's face.

Half a second later, it was rewarded with Sally's smile. They may have their difficulties, but they were a team.

As Izzy braced herself on the table, Sally squeezed past the bartender and put her arm around her mom's waist. Supporting most of the woman's weight, she began the slow process of leading her mother toward the exit sign.

Sally's feet wouldn't work right, and kept sliding in front of one another, slowing their progress and making it harder for Sally to keep both of them upright. But, the door loomed closer.

In the bar, all was silent as the patrons watched their stumbling path, as they wove their way through the occupied tables. About ten feet from the exit, Sally gave a yelp and jumped to the side. In her efforts to keep her mom in an approximate vertical position, she'd forgotten to watch out for the men watching their spectacle. One reached out and pinched her bottom, giving it a squeeze and a nasty twist. Only able to turn her head long enough to give the guy a glare, she kept on.

Chapter Two

Holding her mom up while using both hands to open the exterior door would not work. Sally propped Izzy against the wall and tried to hold her in place with her hip as she yanked at the door. Izzy began a slow descent to the floor. She likely wouldn't hurt herself at the rate she was falling, but it would be a struggle to get her back on her feet. Sally let go of the door handle and caught her mother under the armpits

As she righted the woman to a mostly upright position again, a hairy arm stretched over their heads. The stench of stale cigarettes overwhelmed Sally's senses, but she'd suffer through that to get out of there. The bartender's hand grasped the door handle and pulled, letting in the darkness and the sort of fresh air. "Good luck, kid," he said. "You're gonna need it."

Sally nodded at him once, then dragged her mother across the sidewalk to where Laura's face was plastered to the back seat window.

Sally hammered on the window to get Laura to unlock

the door for them. Laura gave her a two-handed shrug. What? Didn't the useless kid even know how to unlock the doors? Didn't matter. They needed the car keys anyway; they weren't going anywhere without them.

Izzy never took her purse with her to the bar. She'd left it behind far too many times, losing all her IDs plus any cash or credit cards she had on her. These days, she was smart, she said. She chose pants not so tight that the pocket couldn't hold her car keys. In her other hip pocket, she'd slip her credit card, although she rarely had to pay for her own drinks.

Now, to figure out which pocket held the keys. Shoving her mom against the car and trying to hold her there with her body hindered Sally's skill at patting her mom down.

Again, that stale smell came closer. "I'll hold her up, kid, while you look for the keys."

Sally didn't want this man touching her mother. Thinking quickly, she couldn't see any alternative, short of laying her mom flat on the crumbling sidewalk. "Thanks."

She found the keys right away, in her mom's front, right pocket. Their shape was unmistakable; the trick was trying to ease them out of their hiding place.

Realizing her problem, the guy hoisted her mom by the rib cage, holding her straight up and down. There. Now that Izzy wasn't hunched over, Sally could slide the tips of two fingers into that pocket and start to wiggle out the keys.

"You're not going to let her drive."

Sally didn't know if the man asked her a question or made a statement. Either way, he had a good point. If Izzy couldn't walk, couldn't hold her head up, how could she drive?

"Let's put her in the back seat here. Maybe if she sleeps it off for a bit, then she can drive." The man's suggestion might have been helpful, if Sally hadn't known how her mom passed out for hours when she was like this.

Nodding, Sally used the key fob to click the locks open, then held the back door open so the barkeeper could lower Izzy to the seat.

"Whoa!" He stopped. "Where am I supposed to put her?"

"Laura, go out the other side and get in the front seat. Prop Bethany into the corner to make room for Mom." For once, Laura did as asked without arguing.

After allowing Izzy to flop onto the back seat, the man straightened. "Better put a seat belt on her and on the little one." He stood back and watched as Sally did as he suggested. All the while, he regarded Sally. "How old are you?"

"Old enough."

"Do you know how to drive?"

"Of course," Sally lied.

"Yeah, right." He turned his back. "I don't want to know about this. Gotta go see how much these stinking customers robbed me of while my I was outside fiddling around with your mess."

Easing herself behind the steering wheel, Sally looked at the familiar interior. Except, it didn't look quite so familiar from this side of the front seat. She'd watched her mother do this thousands of times. How hard could it be?

"You're not going to drive this thing, are you?" Usually annoying, this time Laura had a legitimate question.

"Maybe."

"Wake up mom and she'll drive."

Sally looked at her younger sister. "Right. You go wake her and get her up here." Surprisingly, Laura obeyed. Or, tried to. While she rested her head on the steering wheel, Sally could hear Laura's voice in the back, imploring Izzy to wake up and take them home.

After a fairly persistent time for Laura, Sally heard the back door close, and the front passenger door opened and shut. Laura stared straight ahead. "She won't wake up." She turned to her older sister. "What do we do now?"

Good question. Glancing over her shoulder, she saw that Bethany was sound asleep, wrapped snuggly in her own coat, plus Sally's. That reminded Sally. In the struggle to get their mom out of the bar and into the car, Sally had forgotten how cold she was. Now that she wasn't exerting herself so much, the shivering began again. How long did it take for someone to freeze to death? Could she stay like this all night, until their mom woke up in the morning and took them home?

"I gotta pee."

Right. That had been the complaint that drove Sally into the bar in the first place.

"You'll have to hold it while I figure something out."

"I can't!"

A car stinking with pee from a five-year-old was bad enough. How much worse would it be if ten-year-old Laura wet herself on the car seat - the seat where Sally always sat?

"Let me think." It only took two tries for Sally to insert the key into the ignition. She'd watched mom do this thousands of times. Maybe millions. How hard could it be? She turned the key to the right and held it there. There was the sound of the car starting up, then a grinding noise. The latter startled Sally enough that she pulled her hand back to her chest. The grinding stopped. Well, so far, so good.

She put her hands on the steering wheel, near the top. It was a stretch, but her hands latched firmly onto the wheel. Now what?

Straining, she peered over the dashboard. She had a good view of the night sky and the streetlights up ahead, but not the road in front of her.

"I think you have to adjust the seat." At least it was a helpful comment from Laura.

"How?"

Laura shrugged.

Sally jiggled on the seat and bounced a bit. Yeah, maybe if she sort of stood, she could see out the front windshield.

"I think I remember mom fiddling with something under her seat. Remember when she dated that guy, Bennie, and he'd use her car? She hated when he left it so she couldn't reach the pedals." Uncharacteristically, Laura was on a helpful roll. Maybe she really was desperate to pee.

With her left hand, Sally felt under the seat. Her hand brushed stale popcorn kernels, some gravel, candy bar wrappers and something sticky she didn't want to think about. The back of her index finger brushed against a bar that seemed to run the width of the seat. Sally pulled up on it, and her seat shot backwards, eliciting a moan from their sleeping mother. Well, that moved the seat for sure, but the wrong way.

She tried again, raising the bar as high as it would go, then trying to squirm her seat into a better position. Nothing. Maybe if she held onto the steering wheel and pulled. She tried, but with one hand on the bar and one on the wheel, she wasn't strong enough to move herself. "Laura, you'll have to help. Get down here and pull up on this bar."

"Do I have to? I need to pee?"

"If you want to find a bathroom, we have to move this car and I can't do that if I can't see."

Grumbling, Laura positioned herself on the floor of the car, draped over the console, and grasped the bar with both hands.

Sally pulled and the seat came forward.

"Ow! You're squishing me!" Laura let go of the bar and edged herself out from beneath the steering wheel.

"Sorry." This new position helped a bit, but she was still too short to see over the dashboard without straining her head. Making herself as small as possible, Sally pressed into the back of the seat and pulled her left leg up under her. There. If she sat on her leg, she gained another few inches. Not ideal, but it would do.

Where was her brain. Here she was freezing, and she'd not even thought to turn on the heat. She knew how to work it as Mom often got her to do it, especially if she was busy putting on her lipstick.

Soon air blew out of the vents, then warm air.

Mom hated what she called parallel parking and refused to do it. She always looked for spots where she could drive in and out without any of that 'stupid back and forth stuff'. Today Izzy had parked with an alley entrance in front of her. There were no cars parked on the other side of the entrance either, so no tricky maneuverings should be needed to drive off.

Sally grasped the level sticking out of the console and tried to pull it back. Nothing. It was stuck beside the letter P. What did Mom do to get this thing moving?

Yeah, she did something with her feet. Sally knew that the pedal on the left was the brake; everyone knew that. Peeking under the dash, she located it, along with the longer, narrow pedal that must be the gas.

Hanging on to the steering wheel to pull herself as close as possible, and rising up slightly on her bent leg, Sally pressed the gas pedal. The engine revved. She tore her foot away. Then she gently pressed the brake pedal. No sound, nothing at all. Okay, she needed to get used to how these felt. She put weight on the gas pedal again, gently this time. The engine's sound changed but it didn't roar. She tried the brake again, pressing and releasing it several times. Now, what was it Mom did to get this thing moving?

Sally thought she recalled seeing Mom's leg move as her hand moved the lever on the console. But which pedal did she press?

"Come on, let's go!" Laura jiggled in her seat.

Deep breath in. Okay. It would probably be better to try the brake pedal first. What if she used the gas and the car shot forward before she knew how to control it? Clasping the steering wheel tightly in her left fist, Sally pulled herself as far forward as she could. She pressed the brake pedal and kept her foot there. With her right hand, she tried moving the lever again. This time it moved. It slid to the R position. R. Did that mean reverse, a fancy way of saying go backwards? No, they didn't want to go backwards because there was a pickup truck there. It probably belonged to some drunk, bad-assed dude in the bar who'd rip her head off if she banged into his truck.

Keeping her foot on the brake, Sally eased the lever back more. Now it rested beside the letter N. N. What would that be for? No go? She skipped it and aimed for the D. That had to mean drive. Hopefully.

The lever settled itself into the D's slot, like it was meant to be there. Sally relaxed her hands. Oops. That meant that her foot no longer pressed so hard on the brake and the car slowly inched forward.

Sally grimaced. Yeah, she meant to do that, she told herself.

Turning the wheel slightly to the left, Sally slowly, ever so slowly steered the vehicle into the street. Funny. When she saw this car beside others, it seemed small, but from behind the wheel, it seemed like she was driving a tank far too big to fit on this city street.

With the brake off, the car crept along. Bethany as a toddler, could have crawled faster.

"Let's go! I need a bathroom like now!"

Okay, keep calm, Sally told herself. Use your brain. In Health class in school, they said to take a deep breath, then several more when you got anxious or scared and didn't know what to do. You need to engage your brain, and to do that you have to breath.

Sally pushed her shoulders back. Nope, that wouldn't do because she needed to hunch forward to grab the steering wheel. But she could breathe.

Stretching her right foot as far as it would go, she pressed down on the gas pedal. The car shot forward. Both Laura and Sally screamed. The jolt loosened Sally's foot, and without the pressure on the GAS pedal, the car returned to its former sedate pace.

Sally tried resting her right heel on the floor and pressing down with her toes. This meant that she took most of her weight on the hands wrapped around the steering wheel. Okay, she told herself. This was doable.

"Red light, red light!" Laura yelled, holding up her hands as it to stop the car's forward motion.

Sheesh! There was so much to pay attention to at once. She was trying to get the hang of how to drive this stupid car and forgot about anything outside of the vehicle. "Thanks," she said to Laura.

Laura muttered under her breath, but Sally didn't have the time nor the brain power to worry about what she said, with all her effort going into jamming that brake pedal as hard as she could.

From behind came the short blast of a car horn. Had they been caught? Was someone going to arrest her for driving underage? The horn came again, longer this time.

"I think they're trying to tell you to go. The light's green now."

Just as Sally eased her foot off the brake and planted her heel on the floor to push on the gas pedal, there was the sound of squealing tires. The car behind them pulled out into the opposite lane and whooshed by them. Good, thought Sally. She had enough to concentrate on without having to worry about someone behind them.

As the car went by, it flashed its lights over and over. On, then off, then on, and off.

"I think they're trying to tell you something," said Laura.

Couldn't she just come out with it? Sally didn't have time to play guessing games.

"Lights. I think you're supposed to have lights on when you drive at night."

"How do you make the lights come on?"

"Why ask me? I'm just a kid."

Sally shot her sister a look.

Up ahead was another intersection and a yellow light. Sally slowly eased her foot off the gas, the car creeping to the corner. "Quick, look. How do we turn on the lights?" Jerking her head around, Sally saw that there was no one behind her. No traffic at all in sight. She could take a few minutes to figure this out.

Laura sat on one leg, rocking back and forth. "I really

need to pee." But she at least looked at the driver's area. After only a few seconds, she pointed. "There. Is that supposed to be a picture of a light bulb?"

Finding the area Laura meant, Sally turned the knob one way, then the other. The lights on the dashboard lit up and beams of light pointed out in front of the car. Thank goodness.

Sally had concentrated so hard on keeping the car in the right lane, that she hadn't paid much attention to where they were. Up ahead she saw the yellow arches, indicating a McDonalds. Now she knew where they were. Next to McDonald's was a Walmart. Walmart had bathrooms.

The entrance into the Walmart parking lot was on the right. Good. She would not have to cross the road to get there. Carefully, and ever so slowly, Sally guided the vehicle in between two sets of white lines. Well, maybe she straddled one of them, but it was near the edge of the parking lot, with no other cars around. She slumped over the steering wheel, relaxing her arms for the first time in ten minutes.

Beside her, Laura jigged up and down.

"Well, go. We're here. Go use the washroom in Walmart."

"Will you come with me?"

Sally threw her head back against the seat. Now she knew why her mother sometimes muttered, "Lord, give me strength." "Can't you just go by yourself."

"I'm scared and it's dark."

"You want me to leave Bethany and Mom here alone in the dark?"

"Lock the door and they'll be fine. Please?"

Sally sighed and tried pulling the key from the ignition. It wouldn't budge. In her efforts to tug on it, her foot dislodged from the brake, and the car edged forward. Quickly, Sally slammed on the brake, throwing both herself and Laura toward the dashboard.

"I think you're supposed to put the car in park when we stop."

Oh, yeah. That made sense. Laura was on a helpful streak. Keeping one foot firmly on the brake, Sally shoved the lever up to the P position. Tentatively, she eased her foot from the brake. Nothing. The car didn't move. This driving stuff was nerve-wracking.

Laura's jiggling sped up.

Glancing at their slumbering mother and little sister, both snoring quietly, Sally agreed that it might be safe enough to leave them locked inside the car. Both seemed out for the night and it was warm enough in there now that the heat had been blasting at them. Besides, she could use the excuse to stretch her legs; her muscles were cramping from their awkward positions, trying to reach the pedals while hoisting herself high enough to see to drive.

Exiting the car, Sally used the fob to lock the doors, checking again that Bethany and Mom were asleep. "Let's make this fast."

She didn't need to warn Laura. Laura led the way, speed-walking toward the entrance doors. Once inside, she stopped dead, partially dazed by the lights, unsure where to go.

"This way," said Sally, pointing to the sign to the left that indicated the public washrooms.

The lavatory was far from pristine with soap smeared on the counter and faucets, paper towels littering the floor. Laura didn't seem to care. She didn't even take time to lock the stall door before finally letting herself go. She peed on and on and on.

"Hurry up. We'd better get back to Mom and Bethany." There was a rustling of clothes, then the toilet flushed and a much relieved Laura headed for the washroom's exit. "Aren't you going to wash your hands?" Sheesh. At ten, she shouldn't need reminding, should she?

As they walked back to the car, Sally ran over in her mind all the steps she needed to take to get the car moving again. Her right thumb attempted to soothe itself by rubbing up and down the side of her index finger. It was exhausting working out all that had to be done. She was tempted to settle in for the night, all four of them sleeping in the car.

But, what if someone saw them. Was it even legal? Would Mom get in trouble? Would Sally get arrested for being the person behind the wheel? No, maybe they should get home.

Chapter Three

It wasn't quite as hard this time. Sally got the car in motion, and in the right direction. She knew the way home from here since Mom often shopped at Walmart. At least, she thought she knew the way. Things looked different from the driver's seat. And in the dark.

Sally squinted. She'd been telling Mom that something was wrong with her eyes. Not that she *wanted* glasses or anything gross like that, but lately she could not read the board at school. Now, when she needed lots of warning to be able to plan her moves, she couldn't quite see where they were until they were almost right at the street corner. This was exhausting. How come teenagers were always eager to start driving?

The leg she sat on was going to sleep, doing that pins and needles thing. Well, it would just have to bear up. She used her hands on the steering wheel to hoist herself up just a bit higher. There. Now her neck was not kinked at such an awkward position, trying to peer over the dash.

Ah, Value Village up ahead. Now Sally definitely knew

where she was. In two blocks was the police station. Dare she drive by it? Her shoulders slumped under the weight of the decisions. Did they never stop?

Would cops be outside their station? Would they notice someone really short driving by? Maybe they had secret cameras. Nah, probably not. Or, would they? Would they take a picture of her and keep it until she was sixteen and tried to get a driver's license? Spring it on her, like they'd had her under surveillance all along, waiting until she was old enough to be arrested for impersonating a driver.

Maybe they'd feel sorry her, think that she was just a kid and it wasn't her fault that she had to drive her family home.

She unclenched her back teeth as she eased up to the next stop light. This time she braked without throwing Laura into the dashboard. Served her right for not putting on her seat belt when Sally reminded her. As the light turned to red, she let her bottom rest on her leg, relaxing the tension on her arms from gripping the steering wheel with all her might. They had a long ways to get before reaching their apartment building. Then what? It was all she could do to keep this machine in the correct lane. There was absolutely no way she'd be able to back it into their parking spot in the tiny, tight parking lot. Would this night never end?

Ahead, light pooled from the front of the cop shop. Then another thought struck. What if? No, she couldn't do it. But what if she just drove right up to their front door. She could lay on the horn, and surely someone would come out to see what the ruckus was about. Then an adult could take over, someone else make the decisions, someone else keep them safe.

But what had mom always said? If the law or the

government got involved, it would split them up. They'd never see one another again. The three kids could taken into the foster care system and mom, well, mom might get in big trouble for not looking after her kids. Could she be thrown in jail?

But at least in foster care, they'd always have something to eat, wouldn't they? There would always be a safe place to pee. There would be no nasty old man hand on her body. Maybe life would be easier for all of them. At least it would be easier for Sally, not having to be the responsible one.

She glanced over her shoulder at her slumbering little sister. Bethany was angelic in the halo created by the street-light. From her driver's seat, Sally could not see her mother, but she could hear her snores. Mom always snored when she'd had too much to drink. Sometimes she farted, too.

The light turned green. Sally took in a deep breath and squared her shoulders. Hands planted firmly at ten and two o'clock on the wheel, she pulled herself up, balancing on her folded left leg, pressed her right heel into the floor and pushed with the ball of her foot. The car shot forward through the intersection, startling Sally so that her foot jerked from the floor and the car slowed. Okay, she told herself. You can do this. She tried again, but too lightly this time. The car barely budged and the car behind them honked.

Laura made a tsk sound with her tongue and rolled her eyes. "This is *so* embarrassing. Can't you even drive right?"

The police station rolled on by. With a car trailing right behind her, Sally couldn't think of a way to turn in there, even if she wanted to. Oh, some part of her really did want to, but she couldn't do that to their mother. Mom trusted her, needed her to help look after the kids. And her.

Mom would be worth little tomorrow morning and

Sally would have a monumental task trying to get her out of bed and off to work. She hoped they had plenty of aspirin left from the last time this had happened. Mom could not miss work or she'd be docked a day's pay. She'd already missed far too many days. She might even get fired if she didn't show up. Sally's grass-cutting job was definitely not enough to support them.

Funny, but Sally had never noticed how very far away their apartment was. The drive seemed to go quickly when someone else was behind the wheel. But finally, finally, it was in sight.

"Hey, you went right past the entrance." Laura, queen of the obvious, informed Sally.

"Yeah, I know. I don't think I can park this thing in our spot. It involves backing up and maneuvering the way Mom does."

"How lame." Laura sighed and stared out the side window.

But her sister had a point. Now what?

Sally swung the wheel to the right at the corner. Too much to the right and the right front tire hit the curb, then propelled them off, back into the center of the road. Good thing no cars were coming. There was still room to make the turn. Or so she thought.

Yep, there was. Now she'd driven past the parking lot entrance, past the apartment building and onto the side street. Vehicles were parked all along the road on the side of their building. Easing her way along, Sally spied a long open space near the next group of buildings.

Carefully, ever so carefully, Sally steered the boat of a car toward those spots. Surely she could make it. She didn't want to hit the curb going in, because that would mean she'd either have to back out and try again or leave the ass end of the car hanging out in the street. Neither option sounded doable.

Boosting herself up as high as she could, her sweaty fingers clutched the steering wheel. She knew now why these wheels had bumps on them, to prevent your fingers from slipping around and losing their grasp.

Pulling the wheel so that they were now parallel to the sagging fence that ran by the sidewalk, Sally removed her foot from the gas pedal and trod on the brake.

This time Laura's seatbelt kept her in place but didn't stop her from complaining.

Sally rested her head on her hands and let her body sag. Home. They'd made it. And, without any of them getting arrested.

Laura opened her door and stepped out. "Are we supposed to be this far from the curb?"

Sally tilted her head in her sister's direction. Through the open passenger door, Sally could see several feet of the paved road, and the entire sidewalk. "It's fine." She knew it wasn't, but there was nothing she could do about it. The ordeal was over and she was done in.

She shut off the car.

Wiggling, she used her hand to help drag her unresponsive left leg out from under her. Ignoring the pins and needles shooting down her appendage, she used her hand to rub away some of the numbness.

When she thought that her leg would support her weight, she opened her door and touched that foot to the ground. It buckled. Swinging her right leg out of the car, she used that as her pivot point while she worked the life back into her left leg.

Then she noticed her sister. Laura was about fifty feet down the sidewalk. "Hey, where are you going?"

Laura turned around, but kept walking, backwards. "Home. I'm tired."

Sally hunched into the car and plucked the keys from the ignition. Holding them up, she dangled them in the air. "How do you think you're going to get in without these?" The streetlight reflected off the shiny metal.

Reluctance in every step, Laura returned. "Give me those." She tried to snatch them from Sally's hand, but Sally was taller and in no mood to be messed with. "You have to help me get them upstairs." Then it struck Sally. How were they going to do this? They lived on the third floor of a walk-up building. Maybe, just maybe, they could carry Bethany all the way, but Mom? No way.

When she was first learning how to cook and clean, she read a book. It talked about life skills being like how to eat an elephant - one bite at a time. They'd take this step-by-step, too. But she was *not* relinquishing the keys to Laura.

Opening the back passenger side door, She unbuckled their smallest sister and shook Bethany. Nothing. That kid would not be roused once she fell asleep. Sally hoisted Bethany into her arms. Five-year-olds might not be huge, but this one was like a leaden sack. The child's head rolled. Sally bounced her and rearranged her hold until Bethany's head rested on her oldest sister's shoulder.

Turning, she looked at their mother, slumped in the other corner of the back seat. "Wake her up, will you?"

Laura put her head into the car and yelled, "Mom!"

Izzy snorted, shifted her head, then resumed her snoring.

"Shake her to get her up," Sally instructed.

"Why does it have to be me? You know she'll hate

whoever wakes her." Both girls knew this from past experience.

"Would you rather carry Bethany?"

Laura scooted over the seat, grabbed her mom's arm and shook it. "Come on, Mom. Get up." No response. "Mom!"

On the sidewalk, Sally juggled Bethany's weight again. She didn't know how long she could keep holding her. "Leave Mom for now. We'll come back for her."

"Gladly."

Sally staggered as her foot left the sidewalk and met the uneven, patchy grass. She'd have to be careful where she put her feet. Bethany could get hurt if they fell.

They almost made it to the back door of the building. There were seven steps to mount before they reached the door. Sally turned and planted her butt on the second step from the bottom. She was done in. How could she get the child up the next five steps?

Then a scary thought occurred. These seven steps were nothing. They had three whole flights of stairs to navigate before getting to their apartment door.

The chill of the night air and the dampness of the concrete under her started to seep in and Sally shivered. She should have taken her coat back from Bethany. On the other hand, she was exercising hard, and so would keep warm. Wrapping her arms around her burden, she pushed up with her feet. Scraping the front of the flaking concrete step with her back, her butt came to rest on the third step.

This would work. She repeated the process until she reached the stoop with a sigh.

"Give me the keys," demanded Laura.

No way, Sally thought. She didn't trust her sister to take off with them, go to bed, and not come back to help.

Bracing her little sister against her chest, Sally balanced, bringing her legs under her and straightening. She groaned.

"Do you know how unladylike that sounds?" Laura's disgusted comment.

Thanks, Laura, thought Sally. "Here, take her." She tried to pass Bethany's weight to Laura.

"Why do I have to hold her? She weighs a ton. I'm only ten."

True. "Just while I get the door open." This lock was always finicky. She got it open. Leaning her back against the opened door, she reached her arms for Bethany.

Laura didn't complain about passing over the child.

They made their way down the stained, linoleum floor, from experience stepping around the spots most likely to have attracted urine, or worse. Reaching the middle of the hallway, Laura held open the door to the stairwell without having to be asked.

Looking up, Sally counted the steps. Eight stair treads, then a landing. Turn, and another eight steps. That would take them to the second floor. Do the whole thing again, and they'd reach their floor. Whatever possessed Mom to pick an apartment on the top floor?

At least there were handrails. Shifting Bethany so that her right arm bore most of the weight, Sally grasped the railing with her left hand and hoisted herself up a step. Yeah, this would work.

She was sweating by the time she reached the first landing. She shifted Bethany so that the child's legs wound around Sally's waist and Sally's arms cradled the little girl's upper thighs. As long as she leaned slightly backwards, Bethany's head remained on Sally's shoulder. Sally backed up against the wall, letting that wall bear some of both of their weights.

"Come on, let's go," urged Laura. She was already one landing up.

This time Sally used her left hand to support Bethany and pulled them up with her right. Now she knew why Physical Education teachers tried to make them do deep knee bends in gym class. Maybe she should have paid attention to that whole physical fitness thing.

There. They were halfway up. Just one more flight of stairs. Well, two sets of stairs actually, with a nice landing in between.

She lay Bethany on the floor, the child laying bonelessly. Nobody slept the way Bethany did. Except maybe for Mom when she'd been drinking.

"I'm not sure I can do this." Sally hated admitting it, but she really wasn't sure she had the strength to make it up the remaining sixteen steps.

"Are you going to just leave her there?"

Geez. What was Laura thinking? "No. Look, you grab her feet and I'll take her arms. We should be able hoist her up between us."

With a glare, Laura complied. Sally was careful of Bethany's head. On the first step the child's bottom smacked the tread and she made a sound. "Lift her higher."

"I can't."

"Bring her back down to the landing." She thought about it. "You lift her under her knees and I'll grab her armpits."

There. That worked better. They wouldn't injure the little girl, but progress was slow. Gently, they set the sleeping girl onto the next landing, panting.

"It was better when just you carried her," Laura said.

Sadly, that was true. "Okay. I need to catch my breath for a minute."

"We need to hurry up. It's late and I'm tired."

Sally eyed her sister. She didn't have the energy for a retort. Besides, she still needed Laura's cooperation.

Bethany on her back was a different problem. While it was one thing to pick her up from a sitting position, this was much harder. Sally raised the child's shoulders. "Here. You get behind her and prop her up so that I can lift her."

Reluctantly, Laura scooted behind Bethany and held her upper body erect. Then, without being asked, she draped the child's arms over Sally's shoulders.

Wrapping her arms around Bethany's waist, Sally tried to stand. Their combined weights were too much for her legs. Another reminder to practice those deep knee bends. "You're going to have to help. I can't lift her on my own."

The more tired Laura got, the less energy she had to argue. Maybe they should keep her tired more often, thought Sally. Together, they got Bethany into the initial position and Sally ordered her screaming calf muscles to push them higher, one step at a time.

She didn't even realize they'd made it to the top, until Laura opened the creaking door. Sally would know that sound anywhere.

It wasn't far from the stairwell to their door. Bracing Bethany's body against the wall, Sally twisted the key in the lock. With little effort, it opened. Just a few more steps, Sally told herself.

Soon the front of her knees hit the twin bed that Bethany shared with Laura. "Pull down the covers," she instructed Laura. Laura did as asked, then toed off her own shoes.

Her arms shaking from the strain, Sally tried to gently lower the dead-to-the-world five-year-old onto her pillow. Really, she should undress the child and put her into pajamas but removing Bethany's shoes plus her own coat as well as Sally's were as far as Sally's energy reserves went. Before she could pull the covers up over their little sister, Laura was in bed, a nightdress over her head and her arm cuddling the pillow.

"What about mom?" Sally asked.

"What about her?" Laura mumbled.

"How are we going to get her up here?"

One of Laura's eyes opened. "We're not."

She was right.

Sally needed to make an attempt, though.

Ignoring her fatigue and wobbling legs, Sally locked the children in the apartment and made her way down, down, down to where she had left the car.

"Mom! Mom!" Sally yelled and tried shaking their mother. Nothing, not a movement, other than her head lolling with the vigorousness of Sally's shakes. Izzy was passed out. They'd seen this before. There would be no waking the woman, at least not for a goodly number of hours.

Sally shivered. She still had not put on her coat. Well, she'd be inside soon.

She felt her mom's hand. Although she had her coat on and Sally had buttoned it up, her exposed skin was a bit chilly. It wasn't yet midnight and the night would grow colder. Since it had taken all Sally had to get Bethany upstairs, she knew that there was no way they could get Izzy up there, even with Laura's help.

Facing the apartment building, Sally made a decision. Boy, it felt like that's all she'd done tonight.

Turning, she went back to the building, let herself in

and trudged up all three flights of stairs. It was easier without her little sister's weight, but her legs still protested.

Once in their suite, she stripped the bedspread and comforter from her mom's bed. Folding them into a loose roll, she locked the apartment door behind her and made her way back down the stairs, to the car.

Throwing the blankets onto the front seat, Sally reached for the large bedspread. Shaking it into the night air, she folded it in half, then tucked it around her mom, covering the woman from her neck down. Next, she took the comforter, wrapping it around Izzy, raising first one shoulder, then the other, tucking the warm duvet under the her body, hoping that the weight would keep the covers in place.

Drats. She'd forgotten a pillow. For a moment, just a moment, Sally debated going back for one. But, eyeing the angle her mother's head was at, she told herself it wasn't needed. Mom would be fine without it.

While she might have forgotten a pillow, she hadn't forgotten a note. She worried that mom might wake up in the night and not know where she was. Sally taped the note to the back of the driver's headrest. Then she locked the car door. Without looking back, she headed to her own bed.

Chapter Four

"It's time to go, Sally. NOW!"

Sally trudged behind her mother.

"Pick up your feet when you walk. We can't afford to wear out the soles on those shoes."

"I don't get why we have to do this."

"Because I said so."

Sally entered the bank behind her mother, hesitating in the doorway. Her mom's high heels echoed on the polished floor. People spoke in hushed tones. Staff in suits rushed by, giving fake smiles to everyone. This did not feel like a place for a kid.

After giving her name at a high counter, her mother motioned Sally to sit with her while they waited. "They said the assistant manager will be with us in a moment. Huh. Like when is that ever true?"

Sally perched on the edge of a turquoise leather chair. Her heel tapped a rapid rhythm on the shiny stone floor.

"Sit back, Sally, and stay still."

Sally pushed herself back into the chair, the backs of her bare legs making a rude noise against the leather.

"Oh, for…" her mother began, but broke off as a woman approached, a woman whose hair was absolutely perfect. Not a hair strayed from its assigned position as she showed her teeth.

"Good afternoon, Mrs. Ramirez. I'm Ms. Colins, the assistant manager. Would you like to come to my office?" She hardly waited for a reply, before leading the way down a hall. As she held open a door, she looked surprised to see Sally trailing behind. She looked questioningly at the woman taking seat in front of her desk. "Is this child with you?"

"Yes. That's why we're here."

Ms. Colins gave Sally just a half-smile and indicated the second chair in front of her desk. Folding her hands and leaning slightly forward, she said, "I've pulled up your account and everything looks in order. How may we help you today?"

"I'd like to put my daughter, Sally, on my account."

Ms. Colin's smile wobbled. "If you would like her to start an account of her own, that's excellent. We encourage children to start young - builds the saving habit, you know. We have a no-fee plan especially for young people."

"No, I don't want her to have an account of her own. Well, I don't care if she does or not, but I want her put on my account."

Ms. Colin's eyes danced between the two of them. "With all due respect, Ms. Ramirez, being named on an account comes with certain, ah, privileges you may not have thought of." Then she caught on. "If you're worried about possible inheritance issues, we can make her a beneficiary on your account." She swiveled her chair toward her computer. "It will just take me a minute to pull up the forms and print them for signing."

"You don't get it." Sally's mom was definite. "I want Sally included on my account. I want her to be able to write checks on the account. I want her to have online access to pay bills."

"Mrs. Ramirez, surely you realize all that entails. We encourage children to begin learning about responsibility and how to handle money at an early age. But they usually do this with their own money, or a small pool of funds supplied by a parent."

"Do I have to give you my reasons why I want this? Do they have to meet your approval?"

"No!" Ms. Colins sat back, distancing herself from the frosty woman in front of her. "It's my responsibility to bring possible issues to your attention."

"Am I allowed to have whoever I want added to me account?"

"Ye-es."

"Then let's get on with whatever paperwork you require to get this done."

"First, we need a few details. Address." She looked toward the other adult in the room. "Do you share the same address?"

Her mom nodded.

"Sally, what is your date of birth?"

Sally stated it.

"Today! It's your birthday. You're officially a teenager now."

Sally nodded. What was she supposed to do with a statement like that? Wasn't it kind of obvious?

"Well, happy birthday. I hope you're having a wonderful day."

Ah, not so much, thought Sally. I'm here, aren't I? This didn't look anything like what she interpreted as wonderful. But she had learned something. Who would have thought a woman like Ms. Colins could gush?

The papers. They kept coming. And coming. Sally'd seen a show on television when they talked about always reading everything before you signed it. In that movie, a woman get herself in real trouble for not reading what they called the fine print. Well, as far as Sally could see, *everything* was fine print on these reams of paper.

Ms. Colins thrust a pen at Sally. "Sign here." She indicated a line where someone had put a big, black X.

Sally looked at her mom out of the corner of her eye.

"Just do it," her mom said.

Sally picked up the first sheet with sweaty hands and raised her eyes to the first line. She read it. Then she read it again. And, again. Still the meaning didn't sink it. Her face flushed and her moist palms clutched the loosened edges of the papers. She hated admitting that she couldn't understand what she was reading.

This made her feel like in school, in those early grades when she dreaded her turn to read aloud. The stupid teacher would make everyone follow along in the story, making them all take turns reading out loud, in front of everyone. Oh, sure, for some kids it was fine. They could read as good as the teacher. But Sally, not so much. The lines wiggled around; the letters would not stay in place, even when she squinted her eyes. With this every-hair-glued-perfectly-in-place Ms. Colins and her mother glaring at her, all those old feelings from school rose up like bile from her gut. She had to say something. "It will take me a bit to read all this."

"Oh, for…" her mother stopped herself this time. "Just sign the thing." She stabbed a finger at the X. "There!"

"But I haven't read it yet."

"It's just their stupid forms. Sign it."

Ms. Colins, condescension dripping from each word jumped it. "It's our standard bank form for when someone opens an account or signs onto an existing account." She gave a smile that wouldn't fool a one-year-old. "Trust me. You're not signing your life away or giving up your first-born." She and Sally's mom shared a laugh.

Sally's thumb rubbed her index finger – up and down, faster and faster.

Smack! Izzy's hand came down hard on Sally's errant thumb. "Quit that!" Izzy hated Sally's nervous twitch. "Sally, we don't have all day. Just sign the damned things."

So she did. And did and did.

"Can she sign her name to my checks now?" Sally's head jerked toward her mom. What?

Although her head pointed at the adult, her eyes cut to Sally and skimmed the part of her body visible over the top of the desk. "Technically," she said slowly. "Now that we've signed these forms, she could legally put her name on the bottom of one of your checks."

"Good."

What was Mom thinking?

"But," went on Ms. Colins, "some receivers of these checks might be alarmed at seeing a signature that doesn't match the name on the top of the check."

"So?"

"So, if you really want this young girl to be able to write

42

checks on your account, you might consider getting new checks made up that reflect both of your names."

"Do it, then."

Again, what was Mom thinking? "I don't really…"

"Sally, keep quiet. Let's get this over with."

"Certainly, then, Ms. Ramirez." Ms. Colin turned her monitor arm so that her clients could see the screen. Quickly she pulled an assortment of checks, some with landscapes, others with shapes and colors in the background. "Which would you prefer?"

Sally leaned forward in her chair. If she had to be involved, some of these were sort of cool. Maybe she could show the kids at school. "Will it have my name on the top?"

Ms. Colins lips smiled, even though her eyes didn't. "Yes, underneath that of your mother's."

"Which one is the cheapest?"

Sally's shoulders fell. Her mom was never into making things pretty.

"This one." Ms. Colins pointed to a plain grey one. There were a few lines on it, but nothing to catch the eye or the imagination like some of the others.

"We'll take that one."

Ms. Colins picked up the sheaf of papers Sally had meticulously signed, tapping their bottoms on her desk to align them. "If that's all then…".

"That means that Sally now has online access to my account and can pay bills for me?"

Ms. Colins blanched. "Ms. Ramirez, I really don't think that is a suitable activity for a thirteen-year-old."

"I didn't ask you what you thought. I asked you if Sally can pay my bills online now."

Ms. Colins sighed. "Would you like to think about this? We can make another appointment for next week, give you some time to consider all aspects of this. I'm sure that like all of us, you work hard for your money and budget carefully. Children don't have that understanding."

"How long have you known my Sally?"

"Well, well, just a half-hour or so."

"Is there anything illegal about Sally accessing my account online?"

"No, not if we've done the paperwork."

Izzy nodded at the pile of papers. "We have."

Ms. Colins shook her head. "What we did here was for the bank account. That means that Sally here could come into the bank and withdraw or deposit funds. Or she could write a check on your account."

"My daughter is unlikely to come wandering into your bank every time a bill needs to be paid. And I don't want to waste postage on mailing in checks all the time. Online is cheaper. Let's get this done."

"All right." Her fingers flew over the keyboard, the printer spewed out yet more paper, page after page of it. "Do you want her to use your current password or create a new one?"

"A new one, one Sally will remember." She looked at Sally. "What password would you like to use?"

Sally's eyes darted each way, all over the corners of the room, every place but near the eyes of her mother and the woman with the lacquered hair. She only had one password she used everywhere she needed one. She never told anyone, especially the kids at school. It was from an old, anciently old TV show that was on probably before her mother's time. There was a little girl on the show, one that everyone was nice to. She had a doll, one she called Mrs. Beasley. So, MrsBeasley was the password that Sally used.

Ms. Colins interrupted Sally's thoughts. "You realize

that this would mean giving your daughter a bank card. A card that is linked to your account."

"I thought that was the point of why we're here."

Ms. Colins looked like Mom sometimes did when she was trying not to lose her cool. "With this bank card and a personal identification number at a bank machine, or the bank card number and a password, she would have full access to your account."

"Well, duh. That's the whole idea."

Doing her job, Ms. Colins persisted. If she'd known mom, she might have opted otherwise. "Young people can be, shall we say, brash. They haven't developed the impulse control that comes with maturity. Too often, if they see something they want, they go after it, without considering the consequences. Sharing access to your money could put you, and your family, in jeopardy."

"Are you finished?"

Sally knew that tone. She could tell that mom was about ready to blow her stack with this Ms. Colins.

Wisely, Ms. Colins kept her mouth shut, but nodded once.

"Sally's not stupid, you know."

Wow! Had she just heard right? Sally knew inside her head that she was far from stupid, but she hadn't realized that her mom knew that as well. The way she talked to her most of the time, as if she was barely tolerable, and hardly measured up....

Ms. Colins was no fool. She gave up. "All right." From a drawer, she pulled a hand-held machine. With a few taps, it spat out a brand new, shiny, plastic card. At the bottom were raised letters that spelled Sally Ramirez. "Sally, insert the card here." She pointed to a slot at the top of the machine. "Now type in a four number sequence that you'll remember. This will be your personal identification number."

A number that she'll remember? That bubble of panic that had nestled just below Sally's diaphragm made its way higher, growing and filling all the space in her chest cavity so her lungs didn't have room to suck in more air. What if she forgot the numbers? Did that mean that mom would lose all of her money? Would they be kicked out of their apartment? Be like those homeless people living out of grocery carts?

Now Ms. Colins gave instructions. The numbers shouldn't be anything easy to guess like 1, 2, 3, 4 or her birthday or her mom's birthday or their address or phone number.

What was left? Both women stared at her, waiting. Her mom uncrossed her legs then crossed them the other way. Then it came to Sally. A place they used to live. There was a really nice old lady across the hall. She'd make cookies and save some for Sally. The lady lived in apartment 3872. She'd remember that. Those were some of the best times of her life. Back when it was just mom and her one sister, back before Laura got so annoying.

Chapter Five

Twice now, Ms. Colins had pulled back the sleeve of her suit and looked at her bejeweled watch. "Well, if that's all…".

Mom hmphed. She uncrossed her legs and leaned forward. "No, it's not all. I told you I want my daughter to have online access to the account. You've got her started with checks and a bank card but that won't help her pay the bills from home."

"Momma," Sally said, keeping her voice low. Things rarely worked in her favor if she crossed Mom. Not rarely, more like *never*, but she let compelled to try. "I don't need to pay bills. It's okay. The lady said I can come here to withdraw money for you when you want."

Her mother slowly turned her head to regard Sally under lowered brows. She paused.

For once, Sally was grateful to be here, in this austere bank. Surely mom wouldn't really let her have it here, in front of all these people.

"Just how many hours do you think there are in a day?"

Even though her mom looked right at her and asked a question, Sally guessed it might not be wise to respond even though she knew the correct answer.

"Just how. Much. Time. Do you think I have on my hands?"

Again, Sally chose to keep silent.

"Between work and getting there and back and looking after you three kids, I don't get a minute to myself."

A part of Sally's brain, the area Ms. Colins said had not yet gained impulse control, nearly blurted out a question of its own, about what kind of 'looking after' Mom meant. As far as Sally could see, she herself did most of the looking after of her sisters.

"I'm asking you to do one thing, just one little thing to take a task off my hands." Mom glared. "You're thirteen now. It's time you took on some responsibility, learned the ways of the world. You'll be in charge of our budget from now on."

Ms. Colin's chair skidded backward on its wheels as her elbows dropped from the edge of the desk. "Now, Mrs. Ramirez. It is one thing to have a child write the occasional check or withdraw money, but to put someone this age in charge of your family's budget? I really don't think...". Whatever she was going to say next froze in her throat from the look Mom gave her.

"Tell me, Ms...." Mom turned the nameplate on the desk toward herself. "Colins. Do you have children?"

Ms. Colins shook her head.

"Then you have no business in telling me how to raise mine."

The banker sputtered an "Of course." Then she picked up her desk phone and hit a button. "Will you please send one of the tellers in here? I'd like her to help a young girl access an online account for the first time." Turning to Mom she said, "I have another meeting I must attend. Someone will be right here to show Sally how to access your account online and get her password set up." She looked toward the door. "Ah, Paige. Come in. This is Sally and her mother, Ms. Ramirez. Ms. Ramirez would like to share online access to her account with her daughter. We've finished the paperwork. If you would take over from here, please." She stood, after gathering her purse from a lower drawer and a briefcase from beside her desk. "I'll leave you to it, then." And she was gone.

The rest went smoothly, or as smoothly as it could with mom tapping her fingernails on the edge of the desk and huffing. She did that when she wanted a cigarette.

This Paige lady didn't blink an eye when Sally typed MrsBeasley into the password slot. The program wasn't happy, though. She needed at least one number as well. It was hard coming up with a number that she'd never forget, especially with mom's toe tapping the front of the desk, and this Paige chick looking like she wanted to get out of there as well. What to do, what to do? Then she had it. Maybe she could use the same numbers she'd just used for her PIN. That way they'd be easier to remember.

She tried again. MrsBeasley3872. Paige didn't seem to care. She glanced long enough to see that the computer program no longer protested, then showed Sally the home page.

It was filled with numbers, most of them in columns, but not all. It was a jumbled mess of numerals and words. Although she'd gotten better at reading, math was her worst subject at school. It was not that she was dumb, but she had to keep missing so much school, that lessons would go by without her. Important stuff, like the next steps in a problem. When Sally got back to school, she hated looking stupid, so she tried to figure it out on her own, never letting anyone see how lost she was. Sitting here with her mom and this stranger, staring at this maze of a screen felt worse than the most awfullest math test she'd ever had to take. That included the one where she'd been off school for over a week, then her first day back, first period, they threw this quiz at her. Well, not just her, but the whole class. The thing is, everyone else seemed to know what to do.

"Sally!" Her mom snapped her fingers in Sally's face. "Earth to Sally. Pay attention here. We need to get out of here sometime today."

Paige looked from Sally to her mother, and back. Her tone softened. "Here," she said. "Take the mouse." Then she pointed to a tab near the top of the screen that said Pay Bills. "Click here."

Sally did. At least she knew how to use a mouse and scroll. This next screen wasn't so bad. It had more words than numbers. Paige pointed out the list of bills that could be paid. Then she showed her where to type in the amount you were paying, then the date you wanted to pay it.

Sally's eyes filled with alarm. "How would I know what date?" How would anyone know such a thing?

Mom rolled her eyes. "It says on the bill."

She didn't add, "dummy", but Sally could feel the unspoken word. Where would she find a bill?

Without her asking, Paige seemed to get it. "They come in the mail. Or sometimes through email." She glanced at Sally, then averted her eyes. Maybe the vibes coming from Sally were less hostile. "Other bills like rent..." she glanced at Mom who nodded, "don't come, but you just know that on a certain date each month they must be paid."

The panic-filled helium balloon that had settled down

somewhat in her chest cavity filled up again, taking up way too much space. Too much for her to even get out a strangled query. How was she supposed to know this stuff? How'd she ever remember? What if she messed up and they got kicked out of their apartment? She knew that it wasn't much of a place, but it was better than living in their car. She'd heard of people doing that. Bethany still peed her pants sometimes and that would really make the car stink.

Paige squeezed her shoulder, but just gently. "Are you all right?" she asked.

"Of course, she's all right." Mom stood. "Are we done here? I've got things to do."

Quickly, Paige showed Sally how to log out of the program. "Don't ever forget to do that."

Why? If she forgot, would all the money in the account disappear? Sally squeezed her nails as hard as she could into her palms. She'd done this before and knew that the crescent-shaped indentations would remain there for the next half hour. Good. Focusing on that hurt gave her time to blink her eyes hard to fight back the puddles forming there. She would not cry, could not cry. Not here, not in front of Mom.

Paige touched the back of her hand. "Here's my card. Keep this. You can call me anytime during work hours if you have a question. Or if you're not sure, come into the bank and ask for me. I can go over this with you again. I know it's confusing at first."

"We're out of here, then." Mom's back was already through the doorway.

Paige held Sally back with a hand on her arm. "If you're not sure, you can bring the bills here and I'll help you pay them. Just until you get the hang of it." Her smile was nice, the first real one Sally had seen all afternoon.

Sally didn't get that many of those sorts of smiles.

"But mom, I still don't get what you want me to do." Sally heard her voice rising to an unattractive almost whine. She hated sounding like a child.

"Here." Her mother strode to the top drawer of the little desk that supported their laptop. Inside the shallow drawer were scads of pieces of paper - some crumpled, some flat, but in messy heaps.

"Do you want me to clean it out? Throw away all the scrap paper?"

Izzy reached in for a handful of papers, withdrawing them and waving them in Sally's face. "*This* isn't scrap paper. *These* are bills."

"Okay." Now what? "Am I supposed to do something with them?"

"Yes! Pay them." Izzy hissed out a breath as she threw the bills back into the drawer and slammed it shut. "Why do you think we went through that circus at the bank this afternoon? It was not for the good of my health."

Cautiously, Sally re-opened the drawer, the way you would a cage door of a starving animal that might see your fingers as food. She pulled out a few, straightening the stack, turning each one face up. "What does this mean?" She held up one with that had OVERDUE written on it diagonally, in large, red, block letters.

"That one didn't get paid when it should have."

"What happens with it now?"

"You, my dear, will need to pay it if we don't want to have our lights turned off."

Sometimes it was hard to tell when Mom was kidding.

Her face didn't always change. And, sometimes her jokes were funny, but sometimes they were mean. If this was a joke, Sally didn't get it.

"Okay. Like Paige showed me. I think I remember how." She hoped so.

"It might be a little trickier than you think." Izzy flipped the bill over. "There's not enough money in the account to cover it."

"Cover it?"

"Pay it. As in insufficient funds."

"So…." Sally's voice trailed off. She didn't know what to say next. Or do next.

"Look, girl. You're going to have to learn how to juggle."

Juggle? Like clowns did with balls? Or plates?

"Lordy, I don't have time for this. Get a brain, Sally. Juggle *bills*. Figure out which ones have to be paid first, or how to put some money down, to partially pay a bill so the company thinks you're trying. They're more lenient on you that way."

"How do I know which ones to partially pay?" She had thought this would be hard, but it was far worse than she feared.

"I need a smoke." She rummaged in her purse for her papers and tobacco pouch. It was cheaper to use roll-your-owns, although she hated the mess. One of her first purchases at the start of a month was a package of regular cigarettes. But, as the month wore on and disposable income became more scarce, she resorted to her pouch of stale tobacco and made her own smokes. "Grab some paper and come with me. I doubt you'll be able to keep all this in your head, so write it down. I'm *not* going over this with you again."

Settled on the back stoop of the sixty-year-old brick apartment building, Izzy began, while staring out at the mostly empty parking lot. "You can look at the online account to see how much is deposited from my paycheck on the first, and fifteenth of each month. That's the money we have to work with."

Sally wasn't sure what to write down, but her mom glared at her, so she wrote 'first and fifteenth of the month'.

"Each deposit is just a bit over a thousand dollars. Our rent on this piece of shit apartment needs to be paid on the first of every month. That's eight hundred and fifty dollars. The landlord is a dragon; she pitches a fit when I'm even a week late and says that if it happens again, she'll kick us out. She means it, too.

Sally knew that it wasn't a great place to live, but it was, well, home. Where'd they go if they weren't here?

"On the first of every month you need to go withdraw four hundred dollars in cash from the bank machine and give it to me. That's for essential stuff that I pay for."

Sally wrote down '400 for mom'. She thought some, then wrote down '850'. Looking at her paper, she figured something out. "That doesn't work. If you say we have to pay rent on the first, that only leaves one hundred-fifty. But you need four hundred on the first. We're 250 short."

The side of Izzy's mouth quirked up. "Right. You're not so dumb. That's what I mean about juggling. You'll need to hold some back from the pay deposit on the fifteenth to help cover that. The $150 will last the first week, but make things too tight for me the second week. You'll need to figure that out."

Sally felt the way she would if someone plunked her in the grade 12 calculus class.

Izzy continued. "Heat and water are included in the rent, so we don't need to worry about that. Power isn't."

"Power?"

Izzy wrinkled her nose at her daughter. "How did I spawn something like you? Power - like lights and plug-ins and the stove and fridge. How did you think those things worked?"

Honestly, Sally had never thought about it. They just worked when you turned on the switch or knob.

"The power company lets us lag somewhat, but we're already behind two months. Can't risk them cutting off our power. We'd have no way to cook, then."

Not that Mom cooked often, but Sally used the stove frequently, especially when making stuff for the little kids.

"I need gas money to get to work. That's about thirty dollars a week, so $120 a month, at least. Better make that a bit more, like $150. There's oil, too. That thing drinks it."

Sally wrote down '$150 for gas'.

"Then there's my cell phone bill and our internet connection. Oh, and I'm still paying on that laptop."

"What do I write down for those things?"

Izzy's look was scathing. "How should I know? I can't be expected to carry all sorts of numbers in my head. That's why they send us bills. Look in the drawer. You can find all the old bills and get the amounts from them."

"Okay, Mom. What else?"

"We used to pay for health insurance, but I had to let that go."

"Anything else?"

"We used to have cable TV, but had to quit. Now we have Netflix and Amazon Prime. They're both about ten bucks a month."

"Each?"

Izzy looked at her as if that was the dumbest question on earth.

Sally wrote down '$20 for TV'. "Is that it?"

"No, food. You kids eat me out of house and home."

It seemed weird to feel guilty for eating. But Sally did. Hating to ask, she needed to know if she was going to do this bill juggling thing. "How much do we spend on food?"

"Depends on the month."

"How do you figure it out?"

"Depends on how much money there is left in the account at the end of the month."

"But what should I write down?"

"Geez. You can't figure out anything on your own, can you?" She took a deep drag of her roll-your-own, and grimaced at the taste. "I don't know. I don't keep track of all our grocery receipts." She eyed her eldest daughter. "But that's something you should do." Izzy took a guess. "Maybe seven hundred dollars when we're doing well."

Quickly, Sally added up all the numbers she'd been given. She must have done that wrong. Her second and third attempts yielded the same results. "This doesn't add up. There's not enough money to cover everything."

"Welcome to the adult world." She blew out smoke, pursing her lips to make rings, then watching her exhalations drift off in the air. Sort of like her money.

"You'll have to take short cuts somewhere." Brushing off the seat of her jeans, she threw the butt of her cigarette onto the concrete stoop, ground it under her sneaker, then went back in the building.

Sally looked up from her calculations. "But...." She noticed that she was on her own.

Chapter Six

"Quit whining!"

"But I'm hungry." Laura upped the whine factor.

Bethany planted her little body in front of Sally, just looking at her with tears pooling in her deep, brown eyes. At five, she had an excuse; she didn't know any better and couldn't understand. But Laura was ten, almost eleven years old. She should get it. Sally had told her often enough. She was sick of it. If there wasn't any food, there wasn't any food.

"Shut up," she told her younger sister. "Go to your room or go outside. Just go."

"You're mean." Laura stuck her tongue out at Sally. "I'm telling Mom when she gets home."

Bethany nodded her agreement and followed Laura out of the apartment.

Sally went into the bathroom, closed, and locked the door. She leaned her back and head against the door, closing her eyes. Her hands fisted and she fought back the tears. "It's a dog-eat-dog world," she reminded herself, "and ya gotta be tough." Well, she was trying, she really, really was.

Her stomach growled. She lifted up her t-shirt, certain that she'd be able to see evidence her stomach lining gnawing at itself. Mom said that you get used to it, but that hadn't happened yet for Sally.

In Health class at school, they studied nutrition, how kids needed to drink milk and juice, rather than pop, and how certain nutrients were required for proper growth and development. Sally was already over five feet tall, and so didn't have that much growing left to do. But she worried about Bethany. The kid was only in kindergarten. Were they warping her brain by not giving her all of the food she needed? When she was all grown up and suffering from rickets or scurvy or some other such thing, would she blame her oldest sister for not providing her with what she needed to grow, to be healthy?

Sally opened all of the cupboard doors, although she was not sure why. She had their inventory memorized. Every day she kept a careful catalog of their diminishing supplies. Six more days until mom's next paycheck arrived. Would they make it this time?

They were down to five things in the pantry - elbow macaroni, ketchup, salt, butter, and three pieces of bread. Sally spread all these ingredients on the counter, planning what to do. She took the plastic bottle of ketchup into the bedroom and hid it at the back of her sock and underwear drawer. If the kids saw it, they'd want some, and it needed to be saved for another meal, one where they'd eat ketchup and bread. She'd have to figure out how to divide the three slices of bread between the four of them.

For tonight's meal, they'd have boiled macaroni with butter and salt. Thank goodness the water bill was paid up so there was plenty of water with which to boil the pasta. This would be their last meal with butter though.

Despite telling Laura and Bethany over and over to be sparing with how much they used, they didn't listen. Maybe Bethany forgot because she was so little, but Laura should know better. When Sally was her age, just a little over two years ago, she'd known. She got it, all right.

She'd seen Mom decline to eat, saying she wasn't hungry, that the girls could have her share. Then, after they'd finished, Sally watched Mom at the kitchen sink, fiercely shoveling into her mouth any little scraps the kids had left on their plates. She'd watched Mom stumble when she walked, and she hadn't even been drinking.

Sally knew that without Mom, they'd be in worse trouble. Mom had to keep working and to do that, she needed to eat to stay healthy enough. Once Sally realized that Mom was passing up food so that her daughters could eat, Sally began eating only a portion of her food, ensuring that some was left for Mom. She tried to get Laura to do the same, but she wouldn't.

That was back when Mom cared. Or maybe before she gave up. She still cared, surely she did. But when things seemed the most hopeless, Izzy drank. Sally hated that. First, she hated how helpless their mother got when drunk - like she couldn't walk right, talk right, or think. All she wanted to do was sleep, even when the little kids needed her attention. Even when Sally had homework to do, when she was just so sick of being the responsible one and wanted to be a kid, even for an hour or two.

Second, Sally hated the money that Izzy spent on booze. They needed that money, needed every penny her paycheck brought in. They couldn't afford the thirty dollars here and there for something as lacking in nutrition as gin or vodka, something that would fill just one of their bellies. But, when things got bad, their mother drank.

Then there'd be more work for Sally. Like trying to get Izzy up on time, dressed, and looking as presentable as a thirty-something hung over woman could look. Izzy could *not* get fired from her job. What would become of them then?

Sally took care and boiled the pasta just right. She followed the timing on the package to the second. She'd learned that mushy pasta got eaten too quickly. Once it became soupy, the kids smashed it around their plates, wasting some of their precious food. Bethany could be excused; she was too young to understand and she wasn't coordinated enough to get the sloppy stuff into her mouth.

Pasta al dente took more work to eat. And, more time. That gave the illusion of the food being more substantial than it actually was. So, Sally had perfected cooking it just the right amount of time.

So that Laura wouldn't hog it all, Sally scraped every last fragment from the butter dish into the warm pasta, mixing it well. There. Everyone would get their share. Checking the salt shaker, she saw that they were okay for a while. She could let everyone put on their own salt. They'd run out of pepper last month, but when she saw how expensive a package was in the supermarket, she'd passed it by. Maybe one day she could buy some as a treat.

Sally knew that Laura would complain about the lack of ketchup. That girl liked to slather the condiment on her plate. Sally wouldn't mind so much if the kid ate it, but she left about half of it behind each time. Each wasted table-spoon added up. Sally had tried to scoop the remnants back into the ketchup bottle, but Laura smeared other gunk into the pile of ketchup, making it impossible to only get pristine red stuff back into the bottle. It was Mom who'd notice the bits coming out of the ketchup bottle that week, exclaiming how gross it was and tossing the whole bottle in the trash. Sally had to wait until everyone was asleep to creep back into the kitchen, retrieve the ketchup bottle from the grimy trash and try to pour it into a clean bowl. Then, she'd spooned out any offending, non-red bits as carefully as she could, before drip by drip, feeding the remainder back into the ketchup bottle.

Now, Sally pulled out her special treat, held in reserve for just such an occasion. Pulling over a chair, she climbed up onto the counter. Balancing on the ledge, she raised herself until she could reach the dusty, greasy space between the top of the upper cupboards and the ceiling. There. Her fingers felt it. A package of dried parsley, or really, the remnants of a package. There wasn't much left, maybe a couple of teaspoonfuls but it would do.

Carefully climbing down, and checking to see that no one was watching, she wiped the dusty plastic package on her shirt, then opened the top. Eyeing it, she saw that the dust and grime had not penetrated the inside. Licking her middle finger, she stuck it inside, then brought the finger to her tongue. She frowned. Nothing. She repeated the action. Hmm. Still no taste. But, no taste was better than an off taste. Maybe the stuff was stale, but it would still look pretty. A garnish, they called it on television.

Proudly presenting the pasta in their one and only serving bowl, Sally set it on the center of the little table that adjoined their galley kitchen. She called out, "Supper." Hastily, before anyone entered the room, she sprinkled what remained of the parsley packet onto the pasta, admiring how the dull green perked up the monotone macaroni.

She seated herself and waited for her family to arrive.

The kids did within seconds. "I'm *starving*," Laura notified the world.

"Me, too." Bethany was far less melodramatic than her sister.

"Sally, you'll have to learn to time things better," Izzy told her oldest daughter. "I'd just settled into my nap when you bellowed."

"Sorry, Mom."

"What's this?" Izzy asked.

"Pasta."

"Didn't we have that last night?"

"Yeah," interrupted Bethany. "But it was red that time."

Izzy could never be harsh with her youngest. "That red stuff was tomato sauce, baby."

Sort of, thought Sally.

As Laura pulled the bowl toward herself, Sally kicked her under the table. "Let Mom and Bethany go first," she prodded.

Laura pouted.

The rest ignored her.

"Can I serve you, baby?" Izzy spooned some onto Bethany's plate.

"I don't want that green stuff. It looks icky. Get it off!" Bethany really could be a baby sometimes.

Sally held out her plate. "Put the green stuff on mine. I don't mind." No kidding, she didn't mind. She'd been saving it up for just such a time as this, when they were all out of other things to put on their macaroni. She thought it looked pretty, fit for one of those cooking contest shows.

One by one, Bethany used her fingers to offload any offending elbow macaroni that had been tainted by the dried parsley.

"Now that you've had yours it's my turn." Laura grabbed the bowl.

Sally looked at her plate. It held only a dozen or so isolated pieces of macaroni, those Bethany had deigned to give her. Sally looked at their mother, seeing if she'd interfere.

Izzy sat with her fork in one hand, her phone in the other. She absently forked in individual pieces of pasta as she scrolled through her Facebook feed.

Sally snatched the bowl from her sister, just as Laura was about to upend it onto her own plate. "I need some of that."

"Pig."

"Cow."

"Girls," warned Izzy. They knew that tone.

Laura relinquished her hold on the bowl, allowing her older sister to take a helping.

"I *made* it," hissed Sally.

"Who cares?" replied Laura.

Chapter Seven

The lights were off.

After their macaroni and parsley flake supper, the next evening's meal consisted of bread with ketchup spread atop. Carefully, artfully, she thought, Sally had cut each slice of bread into quarters on the diagonal. That way they had twelve pieces to share between the four of them. Then she'd arranged them on two plates, fitting the points into each other. It looked quite attractive, Sally thought.

But there were complaints, mostly from Laura, of course, but Mom was critical as well. "Is this all there is?"

Yeah, it was all there was for today.

The next day was worse. All day long Laura whined. Bethany cried, saying she was hungry, but she could be excused. Even showing Laura their empty cupboards didn't drive home the point to the girl that there simply was no more food.

In desperation, Sally caved. At noon, she boiled up some of their precious elbow macaroni to serve herself and her sisters for lunch. Her initial plan had been to only offer the pasta to her younger sisters, but once she spooned it onto two plates, her stomach won out over her will power and she rearranged the servings onto three plates, eating with them. Laura complained that there was nothing but salt to go with the pasta. Sally gave her that stare, the one Mom used to quell any protests. To Sally's surprise, it worked, and Laura shut up.

That evening's meal looked at lot like lunch. Identical, in fact. Mom looked from it to Sally, shrugged, then picked away at her food. "Not very appetizing, is it?" was her only comment.

Pasta filled a hole, at least temporarily. After cleaning up the supper dishes and making sure that Mom planned to stay home with the kids, Sally left the house.

She walked the seven blocks to the supermarket, checking every few minutes that her bank debit card remained shoved into the back pocket of her jeans.

The kids needed food. This one-meal-a-day business had to stop. It wasn't good for Bethany's growing brain. Maybe not Laura's either, but Sally had trouble caring about her annoying sister's development.

Grabbing a hand basket, Sally browsed the supermarket aisles. She checked out the shelves and carts placed at the ends that held discounted items. Unless she got them cheap enough, some of the tinned goods wouldn't work. They needed at least two tins of SpaghettiOs to feed the four of them. But every once in a while, she could find one tin at a good price. If she had enough spare cash to buy it, she did, placing it at the back of a high cupboard, hoarding it until she could find it a partner to make a meal for them.

Today, she was in luck. Usually, she avoided the fresh produce department as things there were way out of their price range. But this time there were bunches of blackened bananas on the cheap. Before anyone else could nab them, Sally slid two small bunches into her basket. They didn't look very good from the outside, but Sally had discovered that once the skins were off, you could mash the insides with a fork, then serve everyone several spoonfuls. It was a treat. Sprinkling a pinch of dried cinnamon onto each bowl helped. Thank you, YouTube for the idea.

That reminded her. Sally headed to the spice aisle to see if any were marked down. They were almost out of cinnamon and had used up the last of their parsley and pepper. Mom really liked pepper.

Protein was what they needed. Everything in the meat section was out of their price range. Sally had tried. Buying two pounds of hamburger had seemed like a good idea, once. She was able to stretch it out to make two meals. But the meat cost so much that they ran out of grocery money for the rest of that week. Now, Sally stuck with sandwich meats that were out-of-date, or almost so. They were the ones with bright red or pink stickers on them.

Yes! She was in luck. Some packages of bologna wore the sale stickers she needed. The small size was three dollars. The package that contained almost twice as much cost half again as much. A better deal. But did she have enough money to get the larger amount? She put both in her basket while she thought about it, searching the shelves for other deals.

There was a package of oatmeal, AND chocolate chip cookies for just fifty cents. A pretty good deal. Sally picked up the bag and rattled it. Yep, it sounded like lots of broken bits inside, but some would be whole. Bethany loved whole cookies.

But she'd already picked up a sweet treat with the

bananas. They didn't really need two treats in one week, but it was tempting. She put it in the basket to decide later.

Longingly, she paused by the aisle that held oils. They *never* came on sale, or at least cheaply enough for her to buy. A whole container of olive or canola oil was pricey. It would last a long time, if she was careful, but they'd have to forgo a lot of other things in order to have oil for frying.

Fried bologna was a hit in their house. Getting it browned just right took grease of some sort. Sally moved on to the dairy section and the margarines. Yep, there was some on sale - not as good a price as she'd like, but maybe it was doable. In their house, they called this butter. It was sort of the same color as butter and did the same things. The word 'butter' sounded better, and Bethany struggled to get all the syllables in 'margarine' in the right order. So, butter it was.

In the cereal aisle, she picked up a bag of rolled oats. It filled stomachs nicely. Oatmeal tasted best with milk and brown sugar, but if she made them runny enough, they were okay without any milk. They'd not had any brown sugar in a while, though.

In the bakery aisle, last week's bread was on for half price. Toasted, it tasted good and fresh.

Shopping wasn't that hard; deciding was. Sally envied those people who seemed to just walk up and down the store aisles, throwing whatever took their fancy into their cart. She swore that one day....

While her bank card stayed in her back, right pocket, a mini calculator sat in her left. Standing in what she hoped was an inconspicuous corner, Sally brought out the calculator and tallied the dollar figure of all that she had placed in her basket so far. Maybe there was enough money to get a quart of milk. She'd have to strictly ration it, or Laura would guzzle it all. Mom would like some in her coffee, too. Coffee! Shoot, she'd almost forgotten. Mom told her they were almost out of coffee. Everyone knew that their mother could not start her day without her coffee. Sally had tried spreading used grounds out to dry, then reusing them. Mom knew right off that something was wrong with her coffee and threw out the whole pot. Sally wished there was a use for used grounds since they seemed to acquire enough of them.

Calculating, she thought that she had around four dollars to splurge on something nice. Nope, brown sugar was too much. Maybe a little bit of white, though. She looked longingly at the honey, but it was much too expensive. She settled on a box of sugar cubes as they were cheaper than the smallest bag and a small jar of strawberry jam that was marked down. That came to more than the four dollars, but not by a lot.

Oh, she almost forgot Mom's coffee. She backtracked to that aisle. While she'd love the get the no name, cheap brand, Mom hated it.

When she got to the till, she knew she'd overspent. There was enough in the account to cover her purchases, but she was running close to the line.

Now, there was no power in the house. This planning stuff was so hard. She'd made sure there was enough left in the bank account to put some money toward the overdue power bill. How was she supposed to know that once you owed over a certain amount for several months in a row, they'd shut off your power until you got caught up? How were people to know such things?

It was three days until Mom's next paycheck would be deposited into the bank. In the meantime, no power meant that they all went to bed early; there was nothing to do once it got dark. Their stove was electric, so there was no way to cook food. Good thing she'd bought some bread and jam. Too bad the toaster ran on electricity.

Although these inconveniences brought complaints from her family, the biggest grieve was caused by no access to television. Laura went to a friend's to watch but refused to take Bethany with her.

Mom ordered Sally to phone the power company in the morning and find out how much they needed to pay to get their power turned back on. Sally wondered how she was supposed to do this when the only phone they owned was Mom's mobile and she took it with her to work. Mom's answer was, "Figure it out."

After getting the kids off to school the next morning, Sally gathered up the last six months' worth of power bills. She'd carefully written on them how much of the balance she paid in the three months since she'd taken on the bill-paying responsibility.

She didn't want to ask the secretary in the office to use a phone at school. No way did she want the teachers knowing how badly she'd screwed up her family's finances. Nor did she want to knock on the landlord's door; she was a sour old hag who didn't like her mom, anyway.

Sally trudged to the bank. That nice lady, Paige, was the only one she could think of who might let her use a phone.

Chapter Eight

At eight-thirty, Sally tried the door. Locked, although she could see people moving around inside the bank. Then she noticed the sign on the door. Open from 9:30 - 5:00.

Well, shoot. She was late for school now anyway, so might as well wait. An hour. What could she do in that time? Near the end of the block was a bus shelter with a bench inside.

Thankfully, there was no one else waiting for a bus. Sally spread her power bills out on the bench, arranging them from the earliest one to the most recent. They weren't all there. For the past year, two were missing. When she'd asked her mom about that, Izzy said, "I can't be expected to keep track of everything. They were too depressing to look at."

Sally had to agree; they were depressing. The only positive was that there had been a few months were the bill was up to date. But Mom must have been short the next month, because she only paid part of that bill. The power company tacked on interest for the unpaid portion, then added all of that to the next bill. The interest kept adding up, as did the unpaid portions of the next bills. Now, they were over two full months behind. How would they get caught up?

Sally had been over and over their budget. Mom said that her 400 a month was non-negotiable, the least owed to her for being the sole breadwinner in the family. She also could not do without her smokes and her coffee. She said that taking a bus to work rather than using her car was out of the question.

They could save twenty dollars a month by cancelling their television subscriptions. When she mentioned that possibility, the wailing and fussing by the girls (and by Mom), was too much to be borne. They could cancel the internet, which would effectively eliminate their TV watching, but Mom said no to that, as well. They dared not pay only part of their rent. Old lady Higgins had said that she'd kick them out the next time that happened. Mom said it was not an idle threat; they'd be sitting on the street corner if their rent was late.

That left just their food budget. There was barely enough money to last each two week stretch as it was. If only Mom would be willing to reduce her "fun" money to three hundred instead of four.

"Nope," Mom said. "It's the least I'm owed for all I do for you ungrateful brats. You need to figure out something else."

Sally wished she had someone to talk to about all this. Mom wasn't interested. "I turned this job over to you for a reason. I'm done with it. I've carried you for thirteen years. You're old enough to take on some of the responsibility now. I bring in the money; you figure out what to do with it."

"I'm trying," said Sally, "I'm trying my damnedest, but it's hard."

"Watch your mouth! Yeah, I know it's hard. I've been doing it all your life. Now it's your turn. Teach you some life lessons. You'll thank me one day."

"But Mom..."

"Suck it up, Buttercup." She grabbed her purse. "I'm going out for a smoke."

Swinging her legs as she sat on the bench, Sally thought about last night.

As she had checked out of the store, she remembered to ask the cashier to double-bag her groceries. She'd had bad experiences with plastic bags breaking on the long walk home, and trying to carry stray items in her arms, while looping her arms through the handles of the still intact bags.

When she got home, she rang the bell to get in. No answer. She kicked the door with her foot. Nothing. Mom must have fallen asleep. Setting her parcels on the dingy hallway carpet, Sally rummaged in her front pocket for her key.

Opening the door, she entered their apartment, using her foot to sweep one of the bags inside. "Hey, can I get some help here?"

No response and none of the lights were on. Retrieving the remaining bags, Sally shut and locked the door behind her, then turned on light switch. Nothing.

Right, of course there were no lights; they had no power. It was just reflex to flick the switch on the wall. As her eyes adjusted to the gloom, she spied a lump on the couch and another on the floor. Laura was asleep sprawled on the couch. Bethany was in a ball on the floor, her baby lips slightly puckered and a tiny bit of drool pooling at the corner of her mouth. Sally scooped Bethany into her arms and carried her to the bed she shared with Laura in the second bedroom. She pulled off the child's socks and shoes, debated trying to get her into her pajamas, but decided against it. She covered her with a blanket, and then peeked into their mother's room. The opened curtains let in the glare from a streetlight. The room was empty.

Back in the living room, she decided that Laura was on her own. But where was Mom? She was supposed to stay home with the kids.

Sally had no watch, so had to guess at the time. Hoping that Paige would have more time for her if she was first in line, Sally returned to the bank, her feet dragging. She so hated to ask for help like this.

Although she couldn't remember Mom actually saying the words, Sally knew that they were to keep private stuff to themselves. No one else needed to know their troubles.

They struggled with that with Bethany. Mom constantly told her, "If you're hungry, keep it to yourself." She instructed Bethany to tell her teacher that she forgot her lunch at home. That way, the kindergarten teacher would give her something to eat. It was confusing that Mom seemed to believe this story she'd made up, as if there really was a child's lunch bag sitting at home, forgotten, rather than there being nothing to put in the bag.

As Sally got to the bank, a woman turned a knob on the inside, unlocking it. She smiled at Sally, one of those fake/friendly smiles Sally now associated with banks.

"Our first customer of the day. Good morning," the woman said around white teeth.

Sally nodded, then a finger inside her head prodded her brain to say more. "Is Paige here?"

"Do you have an appointment?"

Sally's shoulders slumped. She'd not thought of that. Mom had made an appointment when they came to get Sally signed onto her account. Of course, you needed appointments for such things. You could not just waltz into a place like a bank and expect people to help you.

"Never mind. I'll see if she has a few minutes." As she started to move away, she turned back to Sally. "What is your name, please?"

"Sally Ramirez." Okay, maybe the smiley woman was not shark-like.

The lady pointed to the padded chairs where Sally had waited with mom before. "Have a seat."

Sally picked at a scab on her knee. She knew where she got the wound. Climbing on top of the counter to reach the stash of spare food she kept next to the ceiling, she knocked her knee on a cupboard door when she heard Laura about to enter the room. Quickly, she pretended to dust the cupboard top. "Gets pretty gross up here, you know."

Laura didn't know and didn't care. She left the kitchen with barely a glance at Sally's efforts.

"Sally Ramirez is here? The child?" Paige remembered the frightened little girl who'd been in here with her mother not so long ago. "Of course, I'll see her. Give me five minutes to re-arrange my schedule. Tell her I'll be out to get her shortly."

Something about that little girl tugged at Paige's heart.

Something about the kid's mother elicited entirely different feelings.

Standing back, Paige observed the young girl sitting dwarfed by the waiting room chair. Today Sally was alone. That could be good or bad. "Sally. How nice to see you again."

"Hi, Paige. I, um, wonder if I could use your phone, please?"

Paige's eyes narrowed and she tilted her head while regarding Sally. "I, yes, that would be all right. But why don't you tell me what this is about?" Turning, she instructed, "Follow me."

Seated behind her desk, Paige waited.

"I have these papers," Sally started. She spread her stack on the desk.

Paige didn't say anything.

"And I need to make a phone call."

Still nothing.

"We don't have a phone at home, just Mom's cell and she has it at work with her."

"Okay." No judgement, just patience. She didn't push her phone toward Sally, either.

The child squirmed in her seat.

"Sometimes it helps to talk things over."

Sally picked up the pagers, holding the sides tightly in her hands. She placed them in the middle of the desk. "I've messed up."

"Do you want me to look at them?"

Sally nodded. Staring at the desk, she said, "I've made a mess of our budget. I tried, but…"

Quickly, Paige thumbed through the sheets. She smiled. "I see that you put everything nicely in order."

Sally returned the smile. At least she'd done something right, small as it was.

"You were in here what, four months ago?"

Sally nodded.

"So going back through these bills, they were in arrears before you took over making the payments."

Sally nodded again. She knew what arrears meant. After seeing the word on several bills, she'd looked it up.

Paige went through each bill again, this time more slowly, reading the items line by line, as well as the notes about payment that Sally had added. "I see that you're quite systematic about writing things down. That's good."

Sally's hunched shoulders loosened just a bit.

"But, honey, you're getting farther behind, aren't you?"

Another nod. "And now they've turned off our power."

It was Paige's turn to nod. "I'm sorry. What's your plan now?"

"Mom said that I had to phone them to see how much I have to pay off before they'll turn our power back on." She went back to picking at her scab. "We can't cook or watch TV or anything."

"Phoning them is the right thing to do. Creditors feel better when they know that you're trying and are willing to work with them." She referred to the notes written on several month's bills. "It looks like you're trying to pay them, but you're falling more and more behind every month."

Yeah, Sally had figured that much out.

"And the interest is making it harder to get caught up."

Paige got it. "How do I fix this?"

Paige held back the retort that came first to her mind. Pay them what you owe them. She tried a gentler approach.

"Why haven't you been paying the amount the statement says each month?"

"Because there's no money to pay it with."

"Why?"

Sally shrugged. "There just isn't, not after I pay all the things Mom says I have to pay."

Paige pulled a fresh pad of paper from her drawer, plus a red and a blue pen. She moved around the desk to take a seat beside Sally. "Sometimes at the bank, we help people with budget planning. Would you like to do some of that with me?"

The first glimmer of hope appeared in Sally's eyes.

"First, write down what you have to work with, how much money comes in each month."

That was easy. "$1406 on the first of the month and the same amount on the fifteenth."

Paige took a second pad of paper and divided it into six columns. She made these headings at the top of the columns:

Date
Bill Name
Bill Amount
Income
Balance
May 1

$1,406

"Now, what are the expenses that come out of those 1,400 dollars?

"$1,40_6_," corrected Sally.

"Good, you're precise." She pointed to the chart she'd created. "On the lines underneath the income, put down the payments you have to make, as closely as you can remember them, along with the date they need to be paid."

Sally worked away at this for a few minutes. Most of the numbers were fresh in her mind from going over and over them so many times.

Paige stopped her when she got so far.

Date

Bill Name

Bill Amount

Income

Balance

May 1

$1,406

May 1
Mom
$400

$1006
May 1
Rent
$850

$156
May 1
Car and gas

$120

$36
　May1-14
　Food
　$200

-$164
　May 10
　Car payment
　$385

-$877
　May 14
　Power
　$101.49

-$978.49
　May 15

$1,406
$427.51

"Whoa. There's not much left over after those things are paid. Did you hold back some from the previous month's income?"

Sally got that it would be a good idea, but so far, it had

been tough to do.

"One thing you've not written down is food. Do you have any idea how much you spend on groceries?"

"Yes." This Sally knew. She kept all their supermarket receipts and added them up. Constantly. She also knew what the ideal was. She started with that. "I looked it up online to see how much it should cost us to eat." She turned her paper over to write down the numbers she knew off by heart:

Food per week by age

5-year-old
   $32
   10-year-old
   $48
   13-year-old
   $47
   31-year-old
   $48

$175 x 2 weeks = $350

"But we don't spend nearly that much. Sometimes I do a better job of planning than others." It shamed her to admit it, but maybe if she was honest, Paige would be able to tell her how to do better. "I'm not consistent. It's between about $150 and $200 every two weeks."

Paige just looked at her.

Casting her eyes down, "Yeah, I know I should be more careful."

"No! Not at all. You're spending far less on food than I would have thought."

Sally beamed.

Paige let her hair fall forward to hide her face. "What are the rest of your expenses?"

It only took minutes for Sally to write down the rest.

Date
Bill Name
Bill Amount
Income
Income
Balance
May 1

$1,406

May 1
    Mom
    $400

$1006
    May 1
    Rent
    $850

$156
    May 1
    Car and gas
    $120

$36
  May1-14
  Food
  $200

-$164
  May 10
  Car payment
  $385

-$877
  May 14
  Power
  $101.49

-$978.49
  May 15

$1,406

$427.51
  May 15
  Food
  $200

$227.51
  May 25

Mobile phone
$70

$157.51

"Ah. That "$157 is what tides you over for food during the first half of the month."

"Sometimes."

Oh, this poor child. But she'd come here for help, not pity. "You see what the problem is, don't you?"

"I don't know how to budget very well. That's what Mom says."

Paige wrinkled her brow. "Au contraire. I think you're doing an excellent job with what you have to work with. Many adults would not have all these numbers at their fingertips."

Sally smiled at the praise. She had not received a lot of that lately.

"The problem," among other things, Paige thought, "is that all your big expenses come at the beginning of the month. If they were spread out more evenly, you'd find it easier to level out your spending."

"Mom says that I have to pay the rent on the first of the month or we'll get kicked out of the apartment."

"I agree. Rent and the car payment are probably non-negotiables. But maybe we can do some re-arranging to make things easier."

"Okay. What do I do?"

"Let's look at this Mom line. $400. What's that for?"

"Mom says it's the least she's owed for going to work every day and supporting us"

Well. Impulse control, Paige, impulse control, she told herself. Watch your words. "What if your mom didn't take the whole $400 on the first of the month? What if she only took $200 on the first, then the second $200 when her next paycheck came in?"

Sally saw the merit in that.

"And what about this $120 for the car. Does that have to come out on the first? What if she took half on the first and the further $60 on the fifteenth?"

Sally did the calculations. "Then we'd still be in the minus on the fourteenth, but at just -$718.49, instead of -$978.49." Just, she repeated to herself.

Paige's mouth tightened as she looked at the figures. The selfish cow of a mother was spending as much on her own pleasure as she was to feed her family. Her eyes narrowed. She'd bet her own next salary that Izzy Ramirez wasn't doing much of the actual feeding. Her admiration grew for the struggling young girl at her side. What a weight to put on a child. Paige had an idea.

Chapter Nine

"Shall we make that call?"

Sally cringed. She knew that was the whole reason she was here, but, well, she was scared. How did you talk to a power company? How did you talk to someone who was mad at you because you owed them money and kept not paying it?

Paige covered her hand and gave it a squeeze. "It'll be all right. Here's an idea. I don't want to interfere if you don't want me to, but I could make the call and explain the situation, then give you the phone to tell them the efforts you've been making to pay down your bill."

Sally's relief was palpable. "You'd do that?"

Paige nodded. "Okay, then?" At Sally's nod, Paige dialed the number listed on the top of the bill. "May I speak to a manager in the payments department, please?"

A manager! Sally's alarm grew at the thought of speaking to a boss.

"Hello, this is Paige Wilson of the Silver Credit Union. I have a client here with a concern about her power bill. Her name is Sally Ramirez. She is a signatory on her mother's account and her mother has instructed Sally to pay all of their bills." Then she added, "She's thirteen years old." She listened. "Yes, that is her correct age. Let me hand you over to her." To Sally, she said, "You'll need to give them your account number." She pointed to it on the bill.

Sally read the number out loud. She could hear tapping on a keyboard.

"Thank you, dear. And, how long have you been handling the bills for your mother?"

"Four months."

"Ah. I see that the account was in arrears before then."

"Yes. Mom said she had problems."

"I can see that." She sighed. "How may I help you today."

"We have no power. You turned it off."

"*I* didn't, personally, but that is something that happens when an account has been in arrears for over six months."

"I'm trying to pay it, but there's just not enough money."

"I'm sorry, honey. It's hard to be without power. What do you think you should do?"

"Mom said I should phone and see what the minimum amount we need to pay to get our power turned back on."

The woman started to say 'all of it', then she remembered that she was talking to a child, a child not responsible for her parent's irresponsibility. "Is your mother there? May I speak with her?"

"No. She's at work. And, she said I'm supposed to handle this, to figure it out."

The poor kid, the woman thought.

Paige signaled Sally. "May I?" she mouthed.

Sally passed over the phone.

"This is Paige Wilson again. I think that part of their problem is the timing of the invoice. Most of their bills come due within the first half of the month. Her mother's paycheck is deposited on the fifteenth of the month, just *after* your bill comes due. Is there any chance that their due date could be pushed back a few days each month?"

There was a pause and some tapping. "Yes. Done."

Sally gaped. It was that easy?

"Good, thank you. Now, back to Sally's question. Obviously, paying off the total balance due is beyond their means today, but what would you accept so that they could have their power restored?"

Sally crossed her fingers on each hand. Then she crossed her legs and her arms. She'd have crossed her toes, too, if her too-tight sneakers would have allowed it.

"I see. Half of the arrears, plus a payment plan to look after the rest." She thought for a few seconds. "Is there anything you can do about the interest that is accruing?" She waited.

Sally pulled the stack of bills to herself. The arrears. She thought that might mean the amount they owed but wasn't sure. She knew what interest was though, and it added to the bill each month, making it seem impossible to ever catch up.

"Thank you. That is very generous of you. These are exceptional circumstances, though, and we have here a young girl who is earnestly trying to do her best. The 150 dollars will be paid today, and I trust that you'll ensure that their power is turned back on this afternoon. It's been a pleasure doing business with you." She hung up and turned to Sally. "Did you get that?"

Sally nodded, then shook her head. Sort of.

"Here's the deal. You need to pay half of your arrears

right away; that's one hundred fifty dollars. Then your power bill will be increased by ten dollars a month until the arrears are paid off. If you make that payment now, your power will be restored later today."

Good and bad news. "But I don't have one hundred fifty dollars in the account to give her." Or, if I do, we'll have no money to buy groceries.

"Would you excuse me for a minute, please?" Paige left the room. She had an idea. If the bank would not help out, she'd loan this child the money herself.

Paige was smiling when she returned to her office. Her manager got it, and even said it made good business sense to invest in this child. She was the kind of responsible, long-term client they'd like to keep. The Credit Union would allow a one-time overdraft of $150, put into the account immediately, with interest at 2.45 percent. There was no penalty for early repayment of the loan. Seating herself, she explained. "We're going to loan you the $150. This will be an official loan," co-signed by me, she didn't add. "Like any loan, there are interest charges. You will be paying an interest rate of 2.45 percent. The loan must be paid back within two years. You will need to make weekly payments of $1.50." She let that sink in. "How does that sound?"

Sally swallowed, trying to choke down the lump in her throat, but she could not stop the tears that welled up in her eyes. "Does that mean that I'll be able to use the stove to make supper tonight?"

Paige nodded, biting the inside of her cheek to refrain from saying what she really felt. "Of course, you're a minor, so you cannot enter into a contract."

Sally's shoulders fell. "But I'm responsible." Or at least I'm trying to be, she reminded herself.

"Is it all right with you if I call your mom and run this by her?"

Sally hesitated. Would Mom be mad that she'd come to the bank to use the phone? What other options were there? "Okay."

"Excuse me, then. I'll be right back."

It took a long time, far longer than Sally thought it should take, almost longer than they'd been on the phone with the power lady. *That* had turned out all right, so this should, too. It had to.

Paige returned. In her hands were more papers. "I emailed the loan papers to your mom's phone. She signed electronically and returned them to me. I've printed them, but we need your signature now." She pointed. "Here, and here, and here."

Sally signed.

Paige placed half of the papers in one file folder and the other in an envelope. She passed the envelope across the desk to Sally. "This is your copy of the loan agreement. Are you straight about how much you are to pay and when?"

"$1.50 a week." She looked alarmed. "*Which* day of the week? I don't remember reading that." She so didn't want to mess this up.

"Monday. Does that sound all right?"

Yeah, that was easy.

Paige showed her the new line in their online account, the one that showed this loan. "You make the payment in the same way that you pay other bills online. Can you show me how you'd do it?" When she was certain that Sally had it straight, she said, "Two more things."

Sally's heart sank. What now?

"Since we're already in your account, now would be a good time to pay the $150 on your power bill."

"Oh, of course." Geez. How could she forget that? It only took a minute to take care of that chore.

"Now, the other thing. I have a proposition for you. How would you like a job?"

Sally was wary. She knew how much time her mom spent away at her job. If Sally needed to work that many hours, how would she go to school plus look after the kids?

Paige continued. "Did you notice our grass when you came in?"

Sally shook her head. She'd had too much on her mind to notice superficial things like grass. Besides, who cared?

"We used to have a boy come once a week to cut our grass. He was thirteen, like you. But he and his family are moving this week. So, we're looking for someone else to look after our lawn for us. Would that interest you?"

Sally tried to think of how big that lawn was. Since she'd never cut grass in her life, she had no idea how long it would take.

Sensing the reason for Sally's reticence, Paige explained. "Blake spent about two hours a week here. The electric mower is stored in a locked shed behind the parking lot. In addition to cutting the grass, he'd sweep any clippings off of the sidewalk, and pick up any trash laying around."

That didn't sound so hard, and two hours wasn't that much time. Laura could look after Bethany; she wouldn't be happy about it, but it was the least she could do.

"Oh," said Paige. "Did I mention that it pays $14 an hour?"

Chapter Ten

"How dare you embarrass me like that?" The ss sound hissed from Izzy's lips.

"What do you mean, Mom?" Sally didn't get it.

"At the bank. You went and told strangers our troubles. How dare you?"

"You told me I had to phone the power company. I had to find a phone to use."

That gave her mother pause. "You could have done it in private, without spilling your guts to the world."

She hadn't, she really hadn't. "I didn't think you'd want me to ask the landlord to use her phone, or the neighbors."

"Damned right I wouldn't."

"I thought about a phone at school, but you said to never let school people know we're having problems, or they might call Child Protective Services and have us taken away."

"Did you have to tell them *everything*? Couldn't you just ask to use a phone in private?"

"It was that nice lady, Paige. The one who showed me

how to do online banking. She asked. She didn't give me the phone until I'd told her why I needed it."

"That's exactly what I mean. Our troubles are private. You don't go spilling your guts to strangers. Do you want to tear up our family? Have your little sisters taken away?"

Well, sometimes she wouldn't mind if someone removed Laura. Sally always tried to be respectful with Mom. After all, where would they be without her? Mom was the sole provider for the family. But not all of this was Sally's fault. Sure, she'd screwed up with the budgeting stuff, but she was just kid and new to this. Besides, what was she supposed to do? "You could have left me your phone."

"Are you talking back to me, girl?"

"No, Mom." She backed down, but was not totally ready to cop to wrong-doing. "If I hadn't gone to the bank, we'd still have no power. It was Paige who talked to the power lady. She got her to delete all the interest on the arrears."

"Think you're fancy now, using all those big words."

"That's what it's called when you're behind in payments."

"Don't get lippy with me, missy."

Sally couldn't stop now. "It was Paige who got the lady to turn the power back on today if we paid half the arrears."

"And just where did you think you were going to get that money from?"

She had her there. "Paige talked to the manager and got us that loan."

"That's what I'm talking about. How do you think I felt to get an email on my phone at work telling me I needed to sign these papers? I was in the break room, having fun with my friends. Don't you think I deserve that?"

Sally nodded.

"I was so embarrassed. I had to leave the table to read the message again. Any idea how shocked I was to hear that my daughter, my thirteen-year-old daughter had applied for a loan without even talking to me first about it? What gall, girl."

"But I didn't. It wasn't my idea. I just wanted to phone the power company like you said, and to see how much we had to pay to get our lights back on."

"Well, what you wanted and what you got are two different things. Now you've increased our debt. How do you plan to pay it off?"

"Putting in one dollar and a half a week will pay it off in two years, Paige said." Sally frowned. "It said that on the papers. Didn't you read them? Paige said she sent them to you."

"Don't you use that tone with me, young lady." She took a deep drag on her cigarette. "Don't expect that buck fifty to come out of *my* spending money."

Sally nodded. "It won't." She was not sure why, but she didn't tell her mother about the grass-cutting job she'd just landed.

The other thing she didn't tell Mom was about the new bank account. Paige said that lots of kids have one and it was a good way to build positive money habits, whatever that was. Best of all, it didn't cost anything for kids under eighteen.

It came with its own debit card, one with the name, Sally Ramirez embossed on it. It had its own online account access, one that Sally checked every day.

Paige had helped her link some of their bills to this account, like the power bill and the new loan payments. Every Monday, Sally went online and made the loan payment from this account. On Paige's advice, she even put in a bit extra. It was fascinating looking at the charts Paige shared with her. If she put in an extra fifty cents with each payment, the loan went down faster, and she ended up paying a bit less interest.

Yesterday, Sally put twenty dollars toward the power bill. If she kept doing that every month, she would eventually make their arrears disappear. At this rate, within half a year, they'd be caught up.

She felt rich. Fourteen dollars an hour was primo. She made twenty-eight bucks a week - a fortune. Now she could buy food. Not a lot, of course, but there would be none of those days when their cupboards were right bare. They would always have ketchup; she already had plans for Christmas. They'd buy the brand advertised on television, not the no-name kind that was the cheapest.

Sally had another goal. In the meat section of the supermarket, they sold these fat packages of red, ground beef. She always sought out the smallest package she could, the one with the lowest price tag. But she'd worked it out. If you bought in bulk, one of those big packages, the per pound price was cheaper. In the long run, you'd actually *save* money by spending more. But to do that, she had to save up enough to be able to splurge on the bulk package. She smiled to herself. By this Friday, she'd have enough to do that.

She needed one other thing. After searching on YouTube for ways to handle bulk meat, she'd learned that she needed to open up that big, dripping package of ground beef and separate it into smaller chunks, each big enough for one meal. But she couldn't just plunk each portion on a plate in the fridge until it got used. It wouldn't keep and they certainly could not afford to let meat go bad. She needed to buy freezer bags. The lady on YouTube said to check out dollar stores for the best deal.

Sally checked it out. They cost a dollar, but you got fifty bags in the box. Good deal! Yes, Friday was going to be a big day.

The other boon to this secret bank account was Christmas and birthdays. *Now*, Sally had some money to buy presents. They might come from dollar or secondhand stores, but there would be gifts.

Chapter Eleven

"Mom, it's Laura's birthday today."

"Um hmm." Izzy didn't look up from her glossy magazine.

"She's thirteen."

"*Yes*, I know. Now, off you go. I'm trying to read."

"But the bank won't be open much longer today."

Izzy turned the magazine face down over the end of the couch. "And why would the bank's hours interest me?"

"It takes a while for them to do all the paperwork to put Laura on the bank account. If we don't go soon, they'll be closed."

"What the hell are you talking about?"

Sally tried to hold on to her patience, but if they dallied much longer, there might not be time. She had been looking forward to this day for the last two years, ever since she realized she would not be chained to this chore forever. She longed for the spare time she'd have once this weight was off of her shoulders. "She's thirteen. It's time to put her on the account so she can take over paying the bills."

"She's a child. Do you think I'd trust *her* with my money?"

"But *I* did it when I was thirteen. It's her turn now."

"As if. Laura doesn't have a sensible brain in her head. Can you imagine the mess we'd be in if she was in charge of the money?" She picked up her magazine. "Things are fine the way they are."

Sally grappled with the fact that her yearned-for reprieve from bearing the bill paying, budgeting and banking burdens would not be over. Today was supposed to have been the day. She'd counted on it.

She'd already talked to the manager about increasing her hours at the supermarket. She was sixteen now. Her current ten hours a week certainly helped, and there were no more episodes of no food in the house, but think of what she could do with the extra money from working fifteen hours. Maybe she could still fit in extra work hours somehow. Maybe she could convince Laura to help more. Fat chance of that. Her mother interrupted her thoughts.

"Anyway, life is about to get easier around here, once Harry moves in."

Sally's head shot up. "Harry?"

"Yeah, he'll be here tonight. Why don't you make something nice for supper, impress him?"

"Harry?"

Izzy looked up from her magazine. She frowned. "Yes. I just said that."

"But who is he?"

"My boyfriend, of course."

Oh, no. Mom had had a series of boyfriends ever since

Sally could remember. Some stayed only a few days, some months. None of them were any good.

"Where will he stay?"

"With me, of course, you idiot. Where did you think he'd sleep?"

"Does he work?" That was the most important question. Many of the men in Mom's life didn't, or didn't for long.

"Sally! That's rude. Don't you dare speak like that to him. For your information, yes he has a job."

"So he'll pay money into our budget?"

Izzy laughed. "He says he'll pay half the rent and all the booze. My kind of guy."

Yep, that was probably true, thought Sally.

A thump accompanied Harry's arrival, then the sounds of a steel-toed work boot kicking the bottom of the door. "Hey, babe, open up," came through the thin panel door.

Bethany reacted first, jumping off the couch to turn the doorknob.

"Whoa," the man said. "Who's this rug rat?" He smiled, though, when he said it.

Bethany's index finger went into her mouth. "I'm not a rat."

He pushed the door open farther and kicked at his khaki-colored duffle bag. "Bring this in, will ya?" Leaving the child to it, he strode fully inside, yelling, "Izzy? You here?"

Bethany yanked on the ropes leading from the top of the duffle. The bag moved barely an inch. She tried again. Next, she hoisted a leg over the middle of the thing. Straddling it, she attempted to ride it into the apartment. Ineffective, but fun.

Izzy came out of her bedroom, mascara wand in hand, face almost fully made up. Her grin couldn't get any wider as she wound her arms around Harry's neck, pulling him close.

Harry's hands settled on Izzy's back, then slid lower. He returned Izzy's kiss with enthusiasm and a groan. "Damn, you're good."

The bathroom door opened, and Laura stood in the hallway eyeing this intruder.

Over Izzy's shoulder, Harry met Laura's direct gaze. "Izzy, how many of these rug rats do you have?"

Izzy turned to see who he was looking at. "Oh, that's Laura." She held out a hand to her middle daughter. "Come meet Harry, your new daddy."

Both Laura and Harry's heads spun in Izzy's direction.

"Whoa, babe." Harry took a step back. "That's moving fast, don't you think? We only met a few weeks ago."

Izzy's laugh was a frail thing, quick to expire. "Well, what would you like them to call you?"

"Do they need to call me anything? Just Harry is good enough."

"Hello, Just Harry," said Laura.

From the kitchen where she listened in, Sally was envious of Laura. She wished *she'd* said that.

Harry's eyes crinkled as he smiled. To Izzy, he said, "I like this kid. Got spunk." He gave Izzy's rear a squeeze. "Takes after her mother." He turned to follow the thumps coming from near the open door to the hallway outside. "Who's the rug rat trying to ride my duffle bag?"

There was the sound of something plastic cracking within Harry's duffle. From around the wall that hid the kitchen, Sally hurried over to Bethany, lifting the child off the khaki-colored horsey before she could do any more damage. Sally's eyes dared Harry to say anything about the ominous crack they'd all heard. "This is Bethany." She kept both arms securely around the little girl.

Harry's eyebrows lowered, and he faced Izzy again. "*Three* of 'em? You didn't tell me you had three kids. Wait! Are there more?"

"Three's enough for me," Izzy assured him.

Sally hadn't moved.

"Sally, bring Harry's things into the bedroom, would you?" Izzy expected her order to be obeyed.

"I'm making supper."

"Well, we all have to multi-task, don't we?" Izzy took Harry by the hand and led him to the couch. Gently pushing against his shoulders, she shoved until he fell into a sitting position. Then she plunked herself on his lap. "Sally, where's the remote control?"

"Why'd you have to bring him here, Mom?"

"We can use the money."

True, but so far, Sally had seen none of his money. "When's he going to pay us?"

"Pay us? It's not like he's paying for services. I'm not a hooker."

Sally's look questioned her mother. "That's not what I meant. You said he'd pay half the rent. That's $425. He hasn't given us that."

"I don't think he's been paid yet."

"He eats a lot."

"He's a grown man. His body needs twice as much fuel as yours and he does physical work all day."

"I thought labor jobs paid well."

"He makes okay money, he says."

"Then shouldn't he be sharing that, instead of eating off of us?" He'd only been living with them for a few weeks, but already Sally could see the strain on their budget. She was spending almost double for food each day. If she didn't cook more, then there was hardly anything left for the girls once Harry and her mother took their servings. Then that Laura would bitch to Sally, as if it was her fault there wasn't enough to fill their bellies.

It was just the two of them, Sally and Izzy, sitting out on the back stoop facing the parking lot, while Izzy had her smoke.

"Why do we need him? We were doing okay before he came." Especially with the money from Sally's two part-time jobs, that is.

"Sometimes you need a man."

Huh? "Why?"

"A woman's not complete without a man."

Sally thought about that. She couldn't really see how her mom was different now, compared to a month ago, pre-Harry.

Izzy noticed Sally's expression. "You don't get it now, but you will when you're older. A woman alone, well, it says something about her."

"Like what?"

"Like she's not attractive, that no one wants her."

"Who cares what anyone thinks?"

Izzy's look said just how naïve her daughter was. "You're too young to understand, but it matters. It does for sure. You're in your own little world, but when you're older, you'll notice the looks, what people say behind your back, what people think of you."

"I don't think I'll ever care about that."

"Yeah, well, I might have thought that, too, at your age. But then reality sinks in as you get older and have responsibilities."

"After Dave, I thought you swore off men." Dave had been with them for close to a year. The pig left his dirty socks all over the place, just dropping them wherever he pulled them off. Sally was supposed to go around the apartment, gathering up all his dirty clothes, even his stinky underwear, and do his laundry.

Only one side of Izzy's mouth turned up. "Dave didn't turn out so well, did he? I admit I made a mistake with that one." The last straw for her was when she caught him trying to crawl into bed with Sally and Laura. Sally had been sleeping, but Laura's body froze, and her frightened eyes beamed like a laser into her mother's, telling Izzy that this was not the first time Dave had availed himself of her daughter. Nope, that had been it. Izzy had endured that herself as a child and would not have her kids subjected to a man's pawing and worse.

Sally waited. She really wanted to understand.

Izzy drew the smoke deep into her lungs, then tipped her head back. Pursing her lips, opening and closing them, she made perfect smoke rings, a skill she'd perfected years ago. "I like to feel pretty. We don't have a lot of money for fancy clothes and hair stylists. But when a man likes me, I feel pretty anyway." She looked at her daughter. "It's important to be attractive. People like you better then, and they respect you. Remember that."

Sally couldn't see why she'd care about such things. Then she remembered Paige at the bank. When Paige looked at her with approval, *that* felt good, like she'd accomplished something.

"Why don't you have a boyfriend? I had lots of boys running after me by your age." She looked Sally up and down. "You're not bad looking, although you could fix yourself up a bit."

"When would I have time for a boyfriend?" Between school and looking after the apartment and the kids, and her two jobs, Sally fell into bed exhausted each night. Rather than proms and dating, her weary mind filled with all the things she should have done, but didn't have enough hours in the day to complete.

"Oh, don't give me that look. I know you think you're run off your feet. Well, that's life, so get used to it."

There was no point in explaining to Mom. She chose not to get it. Long ago, Sally had realized that it was all right if Mom wanted to believe what she wanted. As long as one of them remained practical, then their family functioned. She knew it was important for Mom to believe the picture she painted in her mind. But sometimes, in times like this, when Mom was talkative, it helped to understand why their life was the way it was.

"Tell me more about why we need Harry."

"Life's not fair. It's a sad fact that men earn more money than women. Always. I work myself to the bone and look at the salary I bring in. But men, well, they easily earn half again what I do, maybe double. The kind of jobs they get have high salaries. I work in a nursing home, taking care of old people. Nothing against them, but they're old and they stink. They need their asses wiped, they need to be fed, all tasks that someone has to do. But I get paid pittance for it. Harry works construction, he swings a hammer all day and carries stuff. He makes almost double what I do. Does society think what he does is more important than my job in looking after their parents and grandparents? That's the value they put on things."

"But some women make more money. My teachers must. There are lady doctors and lawyers."

"Right." She drew the word out. "Those are careers that take education, lots of education. That's not within the reach of people like you and me. I'm talking about jobs that any Joe or Jill can get without some kind of fancy degree. Someone like me qualifies for minimum wage jobs or barely above that, but a man with the same education can get a good-paying labor job." Izzy stood up, brushing off the seat of her jeans. "I'm tired of it. I'm sick of spooning pablum into gaping mouths. I'm sick of changing beds with someone in it. I've worked for almost twenty years at one crappy job after another. If I hook up with a guy, he can look after me. I deserve that."

"But you've been with lots of guys, and it never works out."

"Thanks for reminding me." She stretched out a hand to Sally, a gesture as rare as a moonflower cactus's blooms. "I just haven't found the right guy yet."

Part II

Chapter Twelve

"You're leaving us." It was a statement, not a question.

Sally looked up from her packing to see Laura leaning against the door to their bedroom, arms crossed, a scowl on her face.

"I'm moving out, yes."

"Well. Saint Sally is finally doing it."

"What do you mean?"

"Saint Sally is running away."

Sally straightened. "Why are you calling me that?" This made no sense.

"It's been Sally this, and Sally that forever around here. Sally who does no wrong; Sally who does everything." She straightened too, hands fisted on her hips. "What do you expect us to do?"

But Sally, still stuck on the "saint" stuff, wasn't ready to go there yet. "Why would you call me Saint Sally?"

"That's what everyone thinks of you."

As far as Sally could remember, everyone dumped on her. You didn't dump on saints.

Laura continued. "Bethany adores you. Mom thinks you're perfect and treats you like an adult. You have no idea what it's like to follow in your shadow, do you? It doesn't matter for Bethany - she's little and cute and everyone just naturally loves her. And you, you're the person who does it all. You get all the respect. And me, I'm stuck in the middle, the one everyone ignores. I don't count, compared to the oh-so-perfect Saint Sally."

This was weird, but Sally didn't have time for it now. "You'll get your chance to 'do it all' now." She resumed folding her few t-shirts into the green garbage bag serving as her suitcase.

"I can't believe how selfish you are," continued Laura. "Do you have any idea what it's like to be me? Or care? All my life it's been about Sally - Sally the smart one, Sally the responsible one, listen to Sally I'm told. Do what your sister says."

"Yeah, so? Someone had to make the decisions. You were welcome to share the responsibility anytime you wanted to."

Laura rolled her eyes. "You got everything, you and Bethany. She's the baby, so she got all the toys she wanted. Clothes, too. Nothing was too much for Bethany. And you, you got all the new clothes first."

Right, thought Sally. After pouring through the racks at Goodwill and Value Village, she brought home the best buys she could. "They weren't new."

"They were new to you," Laura shot back. "Me, all I ever got were your hand-me-downs."

When you looked at it that way, it was true. Just three years apart, as soon as Sally outgrew something, it got passed down to Laura.

"You're really ducking out and leaving us to fend for ourselves?" There was a quaver in Laura's voice, just a tiny one, but there just the same.

"I'll show you some stuff before I go, and we have an appointment at the bank this afternoon. Paige will help."

"I don't want her help, and I don't want yours. I just want to be a kid."

"Yeah, well, not all of us get what we want."

"You do!"

Sally could not believe what she just heard. "What?"

"You're running off with your boyfriend, abandoning us."

"I've done everything around here for the last 6 years."

"That's what I mean. What are we supposed to do when you're gone?"

Ah, now they were coming to it. This was the Laura Sally knew. "You'll step up and do what's needed."

"But I don't know how to cook!" The whine was there, all right.

"I've tried to get you into cooking for years. You refused."

"Of course, I did. I'd never be able to do it as well as you. Everyone would hate my food, me included. I wouldn't be perfect like Saint Sally."

This was a new side of Laura. All this time, Sally believed her younger sister was just plain lazy. Could she have been scared to try? "You'll learn. When you have no choice, you learn."

"I don't want to learn. I shouldn't have to! I'm just a kid. And I have school."

"You're 16. I've been doing it since before I was a teenager."

"That's what I mean. You've always been so perfect. How is anyone supposed to live up to that?"

It had been a long time coming - it was late, in fact. While her classmates graduated last June, here it was Christmas and Sally was finally, finally, about to get her diploma.

She remembers how things were 6 months ago.

"You know that you've disgraced us, don't you?" Izzy's fisted hands rested on her hips and her face leaned into Sally's.

What could she say? It wasn't as if she didn't *want* to graduate. Who wouldn't want to be out of that place?

The problem was credits. She didn't have enough. Close, but not quite. All year, the stupid guidance counselor had been telling her that if she would only apply herself, she'd make it. Sure. Apply herself when?

She worked 20 hours a week at the supermarket - 2 hours after school each day, then 10 more hours divided between Saturday and Sunday. It was a struggle to get home from work at 5:30, then getting supper ready for all of them before Bethany said she'd faint from hunger.

Sally had tried over and over, to convince Laura to take on the cooking chore, but nope. "Not my job," said Laura. "Besides, everyone'd hate my cooking." The latter was true.

Mom got home an hour before Sally, but said she was too tired to have to do anymore work when she got home.

Sally also tried to get Laura to take over the lawn-care job at the bank, another thing Laura steadfastly refused to do. That was okay; it was something that Sally didn't mind. She took pride in how the property had developed under her care. Each year, Paige found the money for Sally to purchase shrubs and flowers, so over the last 6 years, there had been lots of changes - good changes.

Now, that was coming to an end, too. Laura had the job, if she wanted it. Laura would need the money to supplement their family's income.

Sally started full-time at the supermarket this week; it would cover her portion of the apartment expenses she'd share with Daryl once she moved in. Plus, there would be a little money left over to pay for her community college night classes. With Paige's help, she'd picked out courses that would lead to a certificate in bookkeeping. Maybe one day, she could become an accountant. Paige said she had a gift for numbers (tell *that* to her high school math teacher). Sally liked the way numbers lined up in columns, things adding up top to bottom and across the way they should. At least they did when there was adequate money coming in to balance the expenditures. Sally's part-time jobs over the years had assured that their family's numbers did indeed line up.

But now it was time to move on with her own life. She'd done her duty by her family for most of her life. Laura could take over now.

A stray thought flitted through Sally's mind. It was funny how none of them talked about Izzy taking over. No, that just wasn't the way the world worked, at least *their* world.

Nothing like having everyone PO'd with her. Everyone except Bethany, of course. The 10-year-old clung to Sally, her wiry little arms refusing to let go. "Why can't you just stay?"

They'd been through this over and over. Even her endless supply of patience with her smallest sister matched the too often almost-barren-cupboards of their kitchen.

Bethany tried another tactic. "Why can't I come with you? I don't take up much space. I'll be good."

Not true. She *took* up space and a lot of it. Sally glanced the cramped, messy bedroom the three girls shared. The bulk of the clothes and toys belonged to Bethany.

"I'm grown up now. I have my own life to lead."

Tears welled and spilled over, drenching Bethany's cheeks. "I want to be with you."

"You'll see me lots still. I'll visit and we can go do stuff together."

"But who will look after us when you're gone?"

Ah, that was it. Sally chided herself for being cynical. She knew that her little sister truly did love her; after all, Sally had been a second mother to her all her life. "Mom and Laura will look after you."

Bethany regarded her with skeptical eyes.

The kid was savvier than people gave her credit for. "It'll be fine," Sally assured her. "I've been teaching Laura what to do."

The child's baby blue eyes narrowed, lasering into Sally's soul. But Sally could not weaken, would not. She deserved a life of her own.

It was just Bethany at home. Izzy was beyond annoyed with Sally.

"If you insist on abandoning your family, there's nothing I can do about it," complained their mother. "If you can do that to us, after all we've done for you, then I wash my hands of you." Then she flounced out to drown her sorrows with sympathetic friends at the bar.

Laura had been next. "You're really going."

Sally had nodded.

"You know you're ruining my life, don't you, and you don't even care."

How could Laura's version of reality be so skewed?

"Since this is my last night of freedom, I'm out of here." Laura slammed the door behind her.

Facing their contempt hurt, but Sally had survived hurts before. Facing Bethany was harder.

The child half turned away, the tears still flowing. She turned her face just enough so her eyes could size up how she was coming across.

A cynical part of Sally, maybe the more worldly part, wondered how much of Bethany's expressions were spontaneous and how much calculated. She had everyone twisted around her baby finger - it had always been that way. They catered to her, the cute baby of the family. Sally picked up her garbage bag, twisting the ends into a knot, and slinging the bag over her shoulder.

"You're leaving me here all by myself?" The waterworks ramped up.

Sally hesitated. It was true that Bethany was rarely left alone. But the kid was 10, almost 11. From the time she was 8, Sally had babysat herself, Laura, and baby Bethany on her own. By age 11, she was used to it. Besides, once she left, Bethany would have only Laura and their mother. Sally suspected Bethany would spend a lot more time on her own. Better get used to it.

Hardening her heart to her little sister's sadness or

manipulations, Sally gave one last piece of advice. "Know what Mom told me when I was a lot younger than you? It's a dog-eat-dog world and ya gotta be tough." With that, Sally gave a last glance around the place that had been home for almost half of her life. She hoisted her bag, opened the door to the hallway, then shut it gently behind her, making her way down the stained carpet to the stairwell.

Chapter Thirteen

"Hey, babe!" Daryl's arms enveloped Sally in a tight hug, his hands planting themselves firmly on her backside.

Sally returned his kisses, only able to give him a partial hug as her right hand still grasped the heavy garbage bag over her shoulder. It had been a long walk and bus ride to get here, and her arms ached from toting her load. She wished Daryl would take the burden from her, but he seemed more interested in greeting her. After the leave-taking she'd received from her family, it was nice to be welcomed by someone. At least Daryl approved of her.

"Come in, come," he said, opening the door fully. "Make yourself at home." He didn't take the bag from her, but returned to his spot on the sagging couch. Using the remote to unmute the large-screen TV, he patted the spot beside him. "Come cuddle up."

Sally set down the bag and closed the door behind her. Although she'd been here before, lots of times, in fact, she looked at it through fresh eyes now.

The smell reminded her of mom, a combination of nicotine and pot. But there was an underlying odor of sweat - male sweat, sort of like an old, damp, wool sweater that had not been cleaned in like forever. There was a scorched odor, like someone had let the water boil out of a cooking pot.

A three-legged coffee table held up on one corner by an empty cardboard box sat planted in front of the couch, overflowing with empty, sort-of-stacked pizza boxes and mounded saucers serving as ashtrays.

A dump. That's what the one-room bachelor suite was. A dump. But Sally had lived in dumps before and made them presentable. With their two incomes, there'd be some money to make this place into something.

She hesitated to put her bag down on the grimy carpet. Who knew what had been ground into its fibers? She didn't take her shoes off, either, although Daryl wasn't afraid to tromp on it with his bare feet.

Hoisting the garbage bag a little higher on her sore shoulder, she trudged to the unmade bed in the far corner. Although the untucked sheets were an odd mixture of gray and yellow stains, at least they had to be cleaner than what was on the floor.

Relieved of the weight, she squared her shoulders and looked around. She could do this. Guys cared little about how things looked, but she could get the place into shape. It was her place, well, hers and Daryl's, but no Mom, and no Laura complaining or getting her to do stuff for them.

"Wanna make us something to eat, babe?" Daryl's eyes never left the ball game on the television.

School had never been an enjoyable experience for Sally. It's not that she had anything against learning, and some of it was even interesting, but it all took time. Time Sally didn't have between her jobs and looking after her family.

To her, school was a sign of her failure. She hated the guidance people who told her to apply herself, that she had potential, if she'd only use it. She hated the teachers who handed back papers that said in red, "Good start, but you didn't finish", or, "You can do better than this."

It was true; she believed she could do better, if only there wasn't always so much that had to be done, and so many people depending on her to do it.

Sally had dreaded starting her first class at the community college, positive it would throw in her face the fact that she could do better, that, no matter how hard she tried, she wasn't good enough. Heck, it had taken her half a year extra just to finish her Grade 12.

This might be just a community college, but it was still college, a post-secondary school. Smart people went to college. Some of them would have nothing to do but focus on their studies. How could she ever keep up? It would be just like in high school, with all the other students looking down on her.

Sally would have quit before she even began, if not for Paige. Paige might be a powerful banking lady now, but she still took time for Sally, took an interest in her and encouraged her. Paige would simply not hear of Sally withdrawing her application. "Try it. You'll see."

As usual, Paige was right. Self-conscious about being older than all her classmates during her final semester of high school, she blended into this night class made up of all ages. A few were kids right out of high school, but most were older adults, some even older than her mother. They all acted like they had jobs during the day. They were all here to learn and didn't seem to care about impressing classmates, nor what anyone wore.

This first class was Accounting Fundamentals. Although some of the terms were slightly different, there was little here that Paige hadn't been over with her throughout the last years. The parts that were new were covered well in the textbook and lectures, plus Sally could always talk to Paige when she had questions.

At 13, when Sally had started looking after the family's finances, Paige had helped her set up a simple system. Over time, Paige added in new items and terminology, guiding her into a generally accepted bookkeeping system. While she had single-entry accounting down pat, double-entry was newer, but Sally liked the symmetry of it, the satisfaction when a page came together exactly as it should.

Sometimes it was hard to concentrate at home, with the ball game blaring on the television. Sally found it especially annoying when Daryl snored away in front of the game. When Sally would tiptoe to the remote to turn the set off, or at least down, Daryl would wake up every time, sensitive to the sound level, demanding that she leave his stuff alone. So, bits of toilet paper stuffed into her ears, then a set of furry earmuffs, deadened the worst of the noise.

Sally stared down at her bitten nails and tried to still her jiggling knee as she waited for the instructor to hand back the first assignment of the class. In high school, she'd dreaded such times, hating the way kids turned to compare marks with their neighbors. She'd hurriedly flipped her paper upside down before anyone could see her grade, then slipped the paper inside her desk. Many times, she didn't even glance at the mark herself, not until long after, when she was all by herself, with no one to jeer at her.

She was careful to hide such papers at home as well, far from Laura's prying eyes. Laura who was on the honor roll, Laura who prided herself on her brains. Laura, who said she was going to make something of herself, that she'd never get stuck living like a loser.

The instructor jolted Sally out of her reverie. "I'd like to make one honorable mention. I rarely talk about marks in this class, but something unusual happened with this first assignment. Accounting isn't easy for many to wrap their mind around. Often it comes easier to older people who've been around a bit, who have experience." She paused and surveyed the thirty-six students in the room. "On this assignment, though, the highest mark was earned by a young person, something I don't think has happened in all the years I've been teaching this class. Let's give a round of applause to Sally Ramirez."

Their life became routine. Daryl's job started early in the morning, so he left before Sally was awake. Mostly. She strove to bury her head under the pillows to drown out the considerable sounds Daryl made before leaving the apartment. Goodness, he stomped around worse than Laura when she was in a mood.

The rest of Sally's day was not that different from her old life. She spent her days at the supermarket full-time and working on her course in the evening. She came home, cleaned the place, then made supper. Daryl ate a lot, probably more than Mom, Laura and Bethany combined, so she made the quantities she was used to, but less than when Harry or some other of her mother's boyfriends lived with them.

There were fewer people in this tiny suite to mess it up. Although Daryl was a slob, so were Laura and Bethany. Izzy might not have been so slovenly if she wasn't always so tired from working, she said. That part of Sally's life didn't change.

She still collected dirty socks from piles on the floor, took soiled dishes to the kitchen and washed them. When she suggested Daryl share some of the less frequent chores, like laundry, he replied that his was a much more physically strenuous job than hers, so he was beat after working all day. It wasn't like this was something new to Sally, so she just schlepped the clothes to the shared laundry room and got the job done.

One day on the way home from work, she spied a wooden table on the curb beside the trash can. She got off the bus one stop early and ran back to look at it. Surely, if someone left it here with their trash, they meant to get rid of it. Inspecting the thing, she saw it had potential. There were gouges in the legs and tabletop, and year's worth of imbedded grime, but that could be overlooked.

Pleased with her find, Sally sent a text to Daryl, asking him to bring his truck. It was a beater but had a bed perfect for carting home this treasure.

Daryl's reply took a while to wind its way back to her. "Sorry, babe. I'm out for a few with the boys. I'll be home in a few hours."

A few hours. It'd be long past dark then, and who knew how many people might stop to snag this antique? Grasping the tabletop under its lip, Sally could easily heft that side of it. But she couldn't get all four legs off the ground at the same time. She'd had some vague notion of hoisting the thing on to her back and carrying it home like a tortoise. Not gonna happen.

There was only one way. Balancing the thing on one leg, she spun the table, gaining two to three feet at a time. It was slow, but over the next hour, she made it the three blocks to the apartment building where they lived.

She paused at the steps, wondering how she was going to get it up to the entrance door, but her current plan worked not just on sidewalks, but on steps, too. Sort of. Using her key to unlock the main door, she tipped the table onto its side, wincing as the broken concrete scratched more of the finish. She jostled two of its legs inside the building, then maneuvered the last legs inside as well. Then, tipping the piece of furniture upright again, she settled into her old pattern of inching the table along the hallway.

Once inside their bachelor suite, Sally took a moment to rest. Proudly, she surveyed her find. It would be an excellent place on which to do her homework. Up to now, she'd perched on the bed, using her knees as a desktop. After working at the store all day, being off her feet felt good, but it was hard on her back to read and write hunched over.

By the time Daryl barged through the door, the worst of the grime had been worked off the table. Sally stood back, surveying her handiwork, proud of this marvelous table, this fresh addition to their space.

"Where's supper? I don't smell nothing."

"Didn't you get my text? I asked you to bring home some fried chicken."

"How am I supposed to hear some stupid text coming in on my phone when I'm busy at the bar? I'm starving." He plunked his butt onto the couch and pointed the remote at the TV.

With a lingering, admiring gaze at her new table, Sally moved into the narrow galley kitchen to make Daryl a sandwich.

Chapter Fourteen

While she'd been into it, Sally's enthusiasm waned. "No, Daryl, wait. We need to use a condom."

"Just this once, babe. I want to feel you and not a rubber."

Sally tried squirming her butt more firmly into the mattress, but she couldn't pull away with Daryl's weight on top of her. Oh, well. Just once wouldn't hurt.

One thing her family's experiences had taught Sally was to shop well. She knew every thrift shop around and how to seek the best bargains.

It took several weeks, but she eventually found and brought home two chairs. They were eclectic, but once cleaned and painted, went well with her pride and joy, the table. She discovered a variety of paint can remnants and bought a paintbrush from a dollar store. Carefully spreading out cardboard and newspapers on the carpet, Sally painted each chair with bright colors and designs, letting her imagination run free.

Daryl complained the paints stunk up the place, but Sally didn't care. He said that the chairs looked goofy, but she didn't care about that, either. Now they had a place to sit and eat, like civilized people. No more scarfing food from their laps while seated on the couch. While Daryl complied with her ruling that they eat at the table like human beings, he insisted on turning the TV on so he could watch while having supper.

Her back hurt less these days. Sally was positive that was because of no longer doing homework on the bed but sitting at her lovely table. Her headaches disappeared, too. She thought those improvements would put her in peak physical condition. But they didn't.

She was tired. Work wasn't any harder, and if anything, her studying load was easier, now that her confidence level was up. She was doing well in this class and looked forward to starting the next one in a month. If only this grinding fatigue would let up. Maybe she needed some vitamins or something.

Back home, life continued for Laura, Bethany, and their mother. Of course, it did, but not well.

Laura hated her life. At the top of her list of woes was her face. It had broken out horribly. Angry red pustules erupted at random all over her face. She changed her hairstyle so that bangs now covered the worst of the ugly blemishes on her forehead, but there was little she could do to hide the massive, abscessed zits on her chin.

Ever since Sally deserted them, Laura's face got worse.

Maybe it was the fact that she was so tired all the time; there was just so much to do. Maybe it was the food they ate - mostly fast-food or frozen meals that could be shoved in the oven. Laura had learned that even they weren't fool-proof. They'd eaten their share of scorched dinners and plenty of soggy, undercooked ones, too. Much as she hated to admit it, she missed Sally's cooking.

And, money. There was never enough of it. Things were a bit better now that she'd pleaded with Sally to help them. Now, on the first of every month, money automatically transferred from Sally's bank account to their mother's.

That happened after Izzy absolutely lost it on Laura. Izzy's mobile phone plan didn't get paid, and she was without her phone for almost two weeks. That meant they were all without a phone, as their mother's was the only phone plan between them.

Laura hated that, too. All her friends had their own phones, but oh no, not Laura. It wasn't fair.

Laura had absolutely no idea how Sally kept to the budget she'd set for food. The only answer Laura could think of was that Sally lied. Her big sister had gone back into the old budget sheets and fudged the amount she allotted for food. Once Sally abandoned them, Laura had gone through the entire month's food budget that first week. Who knew that McDonald's meals for three were so expensive?

It had forced Laura to go back to that Paige lady at the bank. She'd hardly paid attention when she and Sally met with her, not truly believing that they expected her, Laura, to actually manage their family's budget.

It was Paige who pointed out to Laura that fast foods and prepared foods cost more than cooking from scratch. She directed Laura to some online sites that had recipes for cooking in bulk, for making soups and other things that Paige said were nutritious and easier on the pocketbook. Yeah, maybe, but they took time, tons of time, and who had nothing better to do than hang out in their kitchen. Besides, there was no room to work in there. The sink and both counters piled high with dirty dishes. How was she supposed to wash vegetables or cut them up? Besides, there was nothing left to cook with. How come the kitchen didn't look like this when Sally was around?

Laura's attitude toward Bethany changed as well. She used to think her baby sister was cute and was all on board with indulging her, at least to a certain degree. Now Bethany irritated her. Bethany skipped through life, expecting everything to land in her lap. That impish smile? Bethany could pull it out whenever it suited her, whenever she wanted something, or wanted to get out of something.

Laura had ordered Bethany to wash the damned dishes last week. They still weren't done. Laura had dragged the kid by the arm over to the sink and stuck her hand in the grimy, cold water. Bethany squealed and ran away, complaining to Mom that Laura was being mean to her again. That started Izzy up again, ragging on Laura's ass.

Life was so unfair.

"Babe, come on over here. Give your old man some cuddles."

Daryl might try to come off as a tough guy, but he wasn't, at least, where Sally was concerned. He liked her attention, and he liked to cuddle.

It was okay. She'd completed most of her assignment and it wasn't due until next week, anyway. Closing her books, Sally smiled to herself. It was so nice to leave her books on the table, instead of having to shove them under the bed each time she stopped working on them for the evening.

She settled herself under Daryl's arm, ignoring the slight, unwashed smell. His hand cupped her shoulder, giving it a squeeze, then moved lower. He hefted her breast in one hand, appreciating its plumpness. Sally winced slightly; they felt tender lately. "Easy," she reminded him.

Paige studied Sally. Once a month, the two met for lunch. Today they sat on a picnic bench in a park near a taco stand. Today, Sally had brought her most recent school assignment so that Paige could see the big "A" at the top of page one. Paige was Sally's biggest fan, proud of the efforts Sally put in, and thrilled to see this young, frightened girl blossoming into a capable woman with so much promise. But was she overdoing it?

Although Sally smiled, her footsteps dragged. She didn't think Paige noticed when Sally rested her head on the table when Paige went back to the stand to pick up more hot sauce. But she did.

Over the years, they'd built up a trust that allowed them to be blunt with each other. Paige felt something between being a surrogate mother and an older sister to Sally. "Are you putting in extra shifts at work?"

Sally shook her head.

"You look exhausted."

"I can't seem to get caught up on my sleep."

"Is Daryl causing you grief?"

"Nah, he's good. I'm just tired."

Paige's eyes didn't leave her young friend's face.

"I picked up some multi-vitamins, so maybe that will help," Sally added. "Or, maybe I'm coming down with something." She rubbed her stomach. "I'm not really hungry and I have trouble keeping food down."

Paige noticed Sally had only nibbled on her burrito. Oh, no. She almost hated to voice the stray thought that flew by, then infiltrated her brain. "You're not pregnant, are you?"

We were careful, always so careful, Sally assured herself. A baby was not in her plans. No way was she ending up like Izzy; she had plans. She was going places. She'd have a career, not just a job.

Only once ever had she and Daryl not been careful. Just that once, in almost two years of being together. Once couldn't do it.

Her life had led her to face facts head on. While looking after her family, there'd been no room for fairy tales, for maybes or what ifs. Sally learned to look at the facts, add them up, then deal with them.

She squared her shoulders and walked into the free clinic. "I'd like a pregnancy test, please," she told the receptionist.

It didn't take long. Within an hour, Sally was back on the street, a sample bottle of pre-natal vitamins in her purse.

Now, not only her steps were weary, but her heart as well. This was not how her life was supposed to go.

Chapter Fifteen

"No! No way, babe!" Daryl was on his feet, his attention finally ripped from the television.

Sally let him rant, waiting him out. It would be so easy to tell him no, she was just kidding. Then take care of the problem on her own. But she couldn't do that, would not.

"How could you let this happen?" Daryl screamed, the words hitting Sally's core like bullets, then ricocheting around inside her, messing up all her innards. She put a protective hand on the small bulge of her abdomen.

She would not back down. Although willing to share the responsibility, she was not in this alone. "Remember that time I told you to wait, to use a condom, but you didn't want to?"

That went right over Daryl's head. "Get rid of it," he ordered. He sat back down, gripping the remote in his fist, and turning up the volume on the television.

No, this wasn't over. Sally stood directly in Daryl's line of sight, blocking his view of the TV.

"Move," he ordered.

Sally didn't. "I'm not getting rid of it. It's not the baby's fault that we were stupid."

"We? Get real." A thought occurred to Daryl. "Did you do this on purpose? Trying to trick me to stay with you, to *marry* you?" He laughed, a nasty sort of sound. "Like anyone's going to trap *me* that way. You might be a nice lay, but you're not *that* good." He shifted on the couch so that he could see past Sally. The game was on.

"Daryl, we're having a baby." Sally's words quiet, but determined. She tried to reassure him, certain that when he got over the shock, everything would be fine. "It'll be all right, I know how to look after kids."

"Does getting knocked up affect your hearing? I'm not having no kid. If you want to stay here, get rid of it. Otherwise, leave." He pointed the remote toward the door. Putting his feet on the coffee table, he settled his shoulders more firmly into the couch and turned his attention to the screen. He was done with this conversation.

Sally knew Daryl, or at least she had thought she did before sharing this news with him. She'd known it could go either way, but she'd thought she'd hoped....

Sally had seen that set to male shoulders, each time one of her mother's relationships was about to end. A man with his mind made up, a man no longer wanting to be part of their lives.

Besides, did Sally want to bring a child into a home where it wasn't wanted? She and her sisters had experienced that all of their lives. No way was she subjecting a child of her own to that.

From beneath the kitchen sink, she grabbed a garbage

bag. Then, she returned to get another one. She had more stuff now than when she'd moved in.

It didn't take long to gather up her clothes, carefully folding them, so they took up as little space as possible in the bottom of one bag. She divided her textbooks and school-work between the two bags; she'd hate the weight to wear a hole in a bag before she got to where she was going.

Looking around, Sally regretted some things. She'd added touches to this place, small touches, but ones that made it more of a home than a bachelor pad where someone squatted. The clean sheets on the lumpy bed came out of her salary, as well as the mismatched plates and cutlery in the kitchen. The slow cooker that she'd saved up for. All the cleaning supplies she'd slowly accumulated. Daryl could have them all, although she doubted he'd use them.

What she regretted most was having to leave her beautiful table behind. Standing at the door with a bag draped over each shoulder, it saddened her to think that out of everything and everyone in that tiny apartment, she'd miss that table most. Not Daryl.

Izzy opened the apartment door to find Sally standing there, two garbage bags by her feet. "I knew it wouldn't take long for you to come crawling back home with your tail between your legs. It's not as easy as it looks, trying to make a living out there." She looked closer at her oldest daughter. "What's wrong with you? Have a fight with your boyfriend?"

Sally shook her head.

"You're not knocked up, are you?"

Sally said nothing.

"No! No way am I raising your brat. I had three of my own to look after and that's enough for me."

Over their mother's shoulder, Laura and Sally's eyes met. They both knew just how much of the 'looking after' Izzy had done.

Izzy continued. "You think you can get yourself in trouble, then haul your ass back home, expecting me to take you in? It's not that easy. You deserted us, stuck me with doing everything. Why should you come running back now, expecting me to welcome you?"

Sally would not beg. She'd ask once, but not beg. If her mother didn't want her, she'd figure something else out.

Laura pushed past their mom. "Good. You're here. You can take care of this stuff - they're all due." She dropped a fistful of bills onto the floor, some with that dreaded, red OVERDUE stamp on them. "Password's still the same."

As if that decided things, their mom and Laura stepped back from the door and returned to what they were doing before Sally's knock.

Bethany raced up for a hug and helped Sally bring in her bags. "Why's this one so heavy?" Bethany asked.

"It has my books for school in it."

"School?" Laura turned up her lip. "I thought you finished Grade 12."

"I did. I'm taking night classes at the community college, working toward an accounting degree."

"Huh," was their mother's comment. She looked toward Laura. "Sally thinks she's getting uppity on us."

Laura said nothing, but again, her eyes met Sally's, this time with a smidgen of grudging respect.

"I'll just put my stuff in the bedroom, then I'll have a look at these bills," Sally said. She entered the room she'd shared for years with her sisters, braced for what she might find. Sure enough, it was as she expected. Only scant inches of the floor were visible through the piles of clothes on the floor. However did they know which articles were clean and which needed to be washed? She sighed, knowing that she'd end up running all of them through the laundromat, then finding a way to sort and store them away. This was no different from the way Daryl lived before she moved in.

Not finding a spot to place her things, Sally dumped the two bags by the bedroom door and retraced her steps to the living room and the corner desk where she'd paid their bills. She gathered up the papers Laura had dropped on the floor, sat in front of the laptop, and booted it up.

First, she checked Mom's bank account; it was in overdraft. She looked closer - they maxed the overdraft out and there were nine days yet until the next paycheck would be deposited. She scowled at Laura. Was this girl not taking care of things?

At least the power was still on, so Laura hadn't messed up as badly as Sally initially did.

Sally organized the unpaid bills, stacking the most urgent ones on top. Yikes! The rent was overdue. How had Laura let that happen? She waved her sister over.

With a sigh, Laura unwound herself from her cross-legged position on the couch and meandered over. "What?"

"Why's this not paid?"

Laura shrugged. "There's no money to pay it."

"But I told you that the rent has to come first."

Their mom let out an exaggerated breath. "If you girls are going to bicker, I'm out of here." She gathered her purse and left the apartment.

"Let me see your budget." Sally waited and waited.

"Fine," huffed Laura. She dug around in the top desk

drawer until she found the accounts book Sally had set up for her.

There was little written in it. Oh, Laura had started out trying to follow Sally's instructions, but she got discouraged when she could not make things balance out. They had more expenses than money coming in, and every month it got a little worse.

"But I was giving you money every month. Where did that go?" It had not been easy for Sally to donate $200 a month to her family's upkeep.

"I dunno. Food, I guess."

"Where are your grocery receipts?"

Another shrug from Laura.

Sally pierced her sister with a glare.

"I stopped keeping them, all right? It didn't do any good, anyway. It costs a lot to eat, you know."

Sally knew, knew all too well.

"If you were short of money, why didn't you keep the lawn care job at the bank?"

"I hated it. I got grass stains on my sneakers, and I broke a nail trying to get that stupid mower started. Besides, it took up too much of my time." She thrust out her chin. "I have to study, you know. I'm going to finish Grade 12 on time, and graduate with my friends."

No one knew better than Sally just how much time all of these things took. She turned back to the computer.

While she maintained a bank account all to herself, at Paige's insistence, she had another one she shared with Daryl. Twice a month, when she got paid, Sally transferred some into the account she and Daryl shared to cover her share of the rent, food and other expenses.

Actually, it was Daryl's account. He'd put Sally's name on it so that she could pay their bills. But Sally had noticed that often, when the rent was due, their shared account didn't contain enough money to cover Daryl's half of the expenses. He'd say he was a bit short that month since he and the boys had celebrated some birthday or a ball game win.

Just last week, Sally had added her share of their monthly expenses to the joint account. Not without twinges of guilt, Sally now transferred that sum of money back into her own account. She'd need that money if she was going to have a hope of getting her mom's bills caught up. Besides, she was no longer living with Daryl. He'd managed on his own before she moved in, and he could do it again now. Plus, he made almost double her salary.

Mom was right when she said that guys had it a lot easier when it came to making money.

It didn't take long for Sally to transfer cash into her mother's account and pay at least the worst of the overdue bills. Hopefully, after one more paycheck, they'd be in the black again, and could start over. But the food budget was out of control.

"Sally, I'm starving," wailed Bethany. Her twelve-year-old self sounded a lot like the six-year-old she'd once been.

Sally shut down the laptop and poked her head into the kitchen. Good Lord! The place looked as bad as Daryl's had when she moved in with him.

Ah, now she knew why their food budget was through the roof. Greasy pizza boxes lay in a haphazard stack near the garbage can. Trash overflowed, showing off bags and cartons from McDonald's and KFC. Frozen pizza and TV dinner containers littered the floor. It looked like every pot, every plate and bowl they owned was dirty, piled either in the sink or on the counters.

A small voice said behind her, "It's bad, isn't it?" Laura.

At least she recognized things for what they were. Her eyes didn't meet Sally's. "I got discouraged. It was just all so much." She gestured at the obliterated counter space. "I didn't know where to begin and when I'd try, they'd just make more mess all over again."

This honest, vulnerable Laura was new to Sally. She put an arm around her sister's shoulders. "I know. It *is* overwhelming." She pulled her arm away and straightened. "We'll fix it together."

Laura back peddled. "No, not me. This isn't my job."

"Well, I didn't sign on for this either, but this is what life's handed us."

Laura still shook her head. "Have you looked in that sink? I'm not putting my hands in that gunk."

"Fine. I'll do that part. You start with the floor." She looked under the sink. "Where are the garbage bags?"

"We don't have any."

Sally tried to hold on to her temper. "Go dump my things on the bed and use those two bags to gather up this trash." Then she added, "And be careful with my books."

It didn't take Laura long to fill both bags with their refuse. "Now what?" There was still a lot left on the floor.

"Take those bags downstairs, empty them into the dumpster, then bring the bags back for another load. We've got to get this mess out of here before I can even start on the dishes."

"Why doesn't Bethany have to do this?"

Good question.

Chapter Sixteen

It was almost like she'd never left. Quickly, the four of them fell into their old patterns. Laura, at seventeen, spent as little time at home as she could. Bethany now had friends of her own and was often gone as well. No one seemed to keep track of the 12-year-old's whereabouts, and she resented when Sally asked where she'd be. And Izzy, well, she did Izzy stuff. At least she went to work most days, and her pay went into the bank twice a month.

But looking over the last year's bank statements, Sally saw Izzy had been withdrawing far more money than she used to. When Sally asked her about it, Izzy explained it was her "fun" money and fun cost more now than it used to.

"You know that if we don't do something, you're not going to have any fun money, don't you? You were close to getting kicked out of the apartment. What would you do if you got evicted?"

Izzy waved a hand at Sally. "Don't get your panties in a

knot. It didn't happen, did it? Besides, now you're here and you'll fix it."

Sally had learned a lot in the past few years. "Are you giving me permission to fix this?"

"Of course. I just want it to all go away. I'm sick of problems and that Laura never could seem to get a handle on things. Not the way you could."

Sally started to explain that it wasn't all Laura's fault, that Izzy gave the girl little to work with. But she could see that Izzy had turned off and gave up. "Okay, then I'll fix things. But, you may not like it."

"Just do it. I gotta go meet some friends now."

Pleased that their mother had never altered her bank account logon, Sally's name was still on it, so she could make the changes that needed to be done. First, she set up a new account, one in her own name. Later, she'd bring Laura in on it.

Next, she set up automatic transfers from their mom's account into this new one that she called Expenses. Every time their mom's pay was deposited into the original account, they automatically transferred the amount laid out in the budget from years ago into the Expense account to cover half of the rent, utilities, food, and other essentials.

What it left in Izzy's account was money that Izzy could use for her "fun". If she spent wisely, it would add up over time in case she wanted to make a bigger purchase.

Sally entered the password to open up her own personal bank account. She set up an automatic transfer into the new, Expense account that would cover half of their apartment's rent and food. She was used to paying about that amount anyway when she shared with Daryl. Now that money would go to help support her mom and sisters.

Starting a new page in the accounts book, Sally set up a new balance sheet, entering the income and expenses.

Laura pretended indifference when Sally showed it to her, but the younger girl's relief poked through. She hated admitting just how worried she'd been, how desperate to find some way out of the financial hole they were in.

But she was a problem. "Mom's going to be mad."

Sally nodded.

As if her older sister didn't get it, Laura explained, "She spends more than this in a month."

"True, she did. But she can't now."

"I'm telling her you did this, not me."

Sally knew that to be true. "It's okay. It has to be done." At nineteen, how come Sally felt like the eldest in the family, by far?

Maybe Daryl hadn't been so bad.

At the least, he mostly paid his share of the expenses. He wasn't afraid to spend money on them - he'd pick up a pizza or Thai food on the way home from work. If they went out to a restaurant, he'd pay. He made almost double what Sally did, so it made sense. Those things helped pad their joint account so that on those times, when he didn't cough up his share of the rent, they had a cushion saved up to meet expenses.

He wasn't picky, either. Cooking for Daryl was easy - he'd eat anything. Not like Bethany and Laura, who whined when a meal wasn't to their liking. Daryl would wolf down any food set on a plate before him.

When Sally lived with Daryl, she had to pick up after herself and one other person. Granted, Daryl was a slob, but over time, she got to know his ways, and anticipated what he might do. He'd always peel off his socks while watching television and drop them on the floor where he sat. Sally kept a cardboard box beside the couch and, over time, trained Daryl to aim his socks at that box. At least then she didn't have to go hunting under the couch to find matched pairs.

Now back home, Sally picked up after Izzy, Laura, and Bethany. And she'd thought Daryl a slob! Maybe mom wasn't so bad, but her sisters were useless with tidying up.

Sally wrote up a chore list. It hadn't worked with Daryl, but it might work now.

It didn't.

"How do you expect me to do all that when I have to study?" This from Laura. "I'm not going to be some high school drop-out or end up in some loser job. I need the marks to get a scholarship to college."

Bethany just looked, then let it roll off her. With a smile, she left to hang out with her friends.

"I work hard all day," Izzy said. "When I'm off work, I'm off. I work eight hours for you kids, then I'm done."

Somehow, none of them remembered that Sally also worked eight hours a day.

Those eight hours were nothing new. Then why did they seem so much harder now? Sally was not a stranger to work, but now she dragged herself through each day, crashing into bed as soon as she could in the evening.

The morning sickness was mostly gone, although Sally had no idea why people called it morning sickness. Oh, if only it happened in the morning. That nausea stayed with her all day and often into the night. She ate dry crackers, until even the thought of just one more made her want to puke, which sort of defeated the whole purpose.

She hadn't even started to show yet, not really. How would she keep up with her life when she got heavy and had to drag a belly around?

Chapter Seventeen

Money. It all came down to money. Always. Sally yearned for a time when she didn't have to worry about money.

Her mother was improvident, never, ever thinking about the future, always out for the pleasure of the moment. Life didn't work that way. Well, unless you had the sugar daddy that Izzy was always on the watching out for.

It could be worse, Sally thought. At least Izzy hadn't brought home a loser in a while.

Sally recognized that tread. When Izzy had something on her mind, some rant, she had a particular stomp to her step. "How d'you get knocked up?"

The usual way, Sally thought. She waited, knowing there was more.

"That's not the worst thing. You did it with no man to support you. How could you let that happen?"

Ah, the same way you let it happen to you. Three times,

in fact. From experience, Sally knew when to hold her tongue.

"How do you plan to look after this baby?" Izzy demanded. "I'm not supporting it. I've got enough on my plate, looking after my own kids."

The nausea was especially bad today. And the fatigue. Most days Sally understood her mother, tried to shield Izzy from realities she would find too harsh to face. But today, her compassion fund was dry. Right now, she felt sorrier for herself than for her mother. "Looking after your own kids," Sally repeated.

"That's right. You have no idea how hard it is, how relentless." She sniffed. "Guess you're going to find that out."

Bracing herself on the back of the chair and the desk, Sally rose to her feet from where she worked, balancing their accounts. "Just how do you look after your own kids?"

"I work hard all day. And the work doesn't end when I come in through this door."

Enough with the delusions. "That's true. The work does not end when you leave the job. I should know."

Izzy, a little less sure of herself now, made a concession. "Yeah, you have a job now, too."

"I've always had a job, since I've been 13 years old - sometimes part-time, sometimes several part-time jobs at once, and sometimes a full-time job on top of a part-time one."

"Oh. Yeah, but those were just little things, here and there."

"They sure didn't feel little when I was doing them, going to school and looking after this place."

"Looking after this place is never-ending," Izzy agreed.

Sally moved closer, into her mother's personal space.

"What would you know about looking after this place? When's the last time you cooked a meal here? When's the last time you've done laundry? Cleaned the bathroom?"

"Don't you talk to me like that, young lady. I did plenty of that when you were young. There was no one but me to do it all."

"True. But then you dumped it on me."

"Everyone has to do their part. You're the oldest. You have to help out."

"Help out, sure. But do it all? That's something else, and I've been doing it all since I was 13!"

"You exaggerate." Izzy turned away, searching through her purse for a smoke.

"Exaggerate!"

"Of course. Besides, I did it all on my own for years. I deserve a break."

Sally bit the insides of her cheeks to keep from saying more. She'd tried, more than once, to make her mother see reality, but Izzy steadfastly refused that version of the world. If Sally pushed too much, Izzy would retreat either to her bed, or stay away for days, missing work while she partied with friends. They couldn't afford for her to be docked pay.

Izzy upended her purse on the coffee table. "There's got to be more here." She rooted around in the mess until she found her wallet. Opening the billfold section, she found a twenty and a ten, plus loose coins in the change purse area. "Where'd all my money go?" She looked accusingly at her oldest daughter. "Did you take my money?"

Sally shook her head. "Of course not."

Izzy let that go. "Must have been that Laura. That child always wants more."

"I haven't seen Laura or Bethany near your room. Where'd you leave your purse?"

"Beside my bed, as usual."

"How much did you spend at the bar last night?"

"How am I supposed to know that? When I'm out having fun, I'm not counting pennies." She stuffed the jumble of items back into her handbag. "You wouldn't want to run out to the bank machine for me, would you? I'm tired and I need a nap."

"Just a minute." Sally sat back down in front of the laptop and pulled up her mother's bank account. "You have a bit you can withdraw, but it looks like you've already spent everything from this paycheck."

"Let me look. That's just not possible." She wasn't sure what she was looking at.

Sally pointed out the balance.

"I make a lot more money than that," protested Izzy. "There's got to be more than that left."

Sally took a deep breath. She really wasn't up to getting into this right now, but they had thrust it upon her. Laura had said Mom would be mad. She was right, but Sally had hoped to stave off the volcano at least until she was feeling better. She pulled out their ledger book from the drawer and opened it to that month's pages. "Here's the amount of your take-home pay."

"Pitiful, the amounts that the government withholds from poor, working people."

"Here are all our expenses - they're totaled here. Then we divide that by two, because I'm paying half of them."

Izzy waved away that last bit.

Sally continued. "So, from your paycheck, we have to take off half of the expenses." She pointed to the computer screen. "See, here is where your check went into the account. Then your half of the expenses were withdrawn." She checked that her mother was paying attention. "What's left is the amount of money you have to spend on yourself until your next paycheck." She rested her hands in her lap and waited.

Izzy stared, then moved her gaze several times between the ledger book and the screen. "But that's not enough to live on. I've spent more on a girl's day out than that."

"I suppose you have," agreed Sally.

"But I don't get paid for another week."

"True."

"What am I supposed to do until then?"

"Like the rest of us - budget and make do."

"After all I do around here, after I put up with that stupid job all week, I can't even go out and have a little fun?"

It wasn't pleasant to see a grown woman pout, Sally thought.

Izzy turned on her daughter. "This is all your fault. Before you brought your tail back here, we were doing just fine. I had lots of money to do the things I wanted to, things I needed to do."

This was going to get ugly. "No, you didn't." Sally tried to keep her voice level. "You were behind in your rent. Other bills went unpaid. This place was a trash heap. Things were not fine."

"It's that Laura's fault. After you ditched us, she was supposed to look after things. That girl is so lazy. She let this place go and she couldn't even keep the bills paid on time. I tell you…"

"No. It was not Laura's fault. You took too much money out of the account, not leaving enough to pay the bills. You almost got yourself evicted."

"It would never have come to that."

Sally just looked at her mother. How could someone of her age be so delusional?

Izzy paced. Some modicum of reality must have penetrated. She lit a cigarette, even though this was a no-smoking building. "You know what the problem is?" She continued without waiting for a response from Sally. "I've been without a man for too long. Men make more money than we do. I don't know what I've been thinking lately, sticking with my girlfriends, instead of socializing." She looked Sally's way, as if expecting an argument. "I've still got it, you know. I can get any man I want, and he'll be begging to move in here, to help with the expenses."

Sally's heart sank. Not again.

Chapter Eighteen

She was not supposed to take phone calls at work, but her phone kept buzzing. When no one was looking, she slipped the mobile out of her pocket. Daryl. Again. She silenced the call. She was through with him. If he didn't want her and the baby, she didn't want him.

Next, her phone vibrated, signaling an incoming text message. From him. "Meet me at Dairy Queen when you get off work. It's important. Darla says to tell you to be sure to come."

Darla. Why would Daryl's twin sister say that? Was something wrong with her? Sally always liked Darla, some days more than she did Daryl.

"What's up?" Sally asked as she eased her swollen belly into the small space between the plastic booth and the table.

Daryl's eyes traveled from her face to her boobs to her abdominal bulge, and back again. "I see you're growing in lots of places." His grin was close to a leer.

"Look all you want, but that's all you're getting. Your choice, remember?"

"I'm not here to fight with you." As a peace offering, he shoved a peanut buster parfait across the table to Sally. Her favorite. He slurped his milkshake through a straw.

There was no distracting Sally that easily. "Then why did you call? You made it clear you didn't want me to have this baby."

"And, I don't. At least I don't want any kid."

Sally hoisted her purse strap over her shoulder. Placing both hands on the table, she pushed herself up. "The kid and I go together."

Daryl placed his hand over hers. "No, wait. I need to talk to you."

Sally puffed out a breath. "Fine. Make it fast. I'm tired and want to get home."

"Darla's been asking after you."

"How is she?"

"She's fine." He looked away. "She said I'm an ass for letting you go."

"Darla always was a smart woman."

"She was riding me for weeks about why we broke up. When I finally told her, she went nuts on me."

That seemed over the top, even if Darla and she had gotten along. "She thought you should grow up and be a dad?"

Darly picked at a fingernail. "Not exactly. She said that the kid might be better off with just you as a parent."

"Huh." Sally leaned back and crossed her arms.

"She said some other stuff." Daryl raised a thumb to his mouth and gnawed on a cuticle, a sure tell that he was uncomfortable. "She said it was one thing if I didn't want to be in the baby's life."

"And you don't." A statement rather than a question.

"No, I don't. I didn't plan on being no daddy. But Darla says I got responsibilities. Even if I'm not raising the kid, I should support it." He hastened to add, "With money, that is."

Well, this was unexpected.

"Darla says that you could take me to court if you wanted, that I'm just lucky you haven't done that." He looked questioningly at Sally. "You aren't planning that, are you?"

Sally shook her head. It had never occurred to her.

"So, here's the deal." Daryl pulled a torn sheet of notepaper from his pocket. "Darla helped me with this. Here's what she thinks is fair." He thrust the paper across the table to Sally.

She glanced down. At the top of the page, hand-printed letters said $400. Under that was a line that said:

- been pregnant for seven months = $400 x 7 = $2,800

Sally's eyes flicked to Daryl's. Could this mean what she thought it did?

Daryl fished in his pocket for his wallet. Withdrawing it, he placed on Sally's side of the table a folded check.

Opening it, Sally saw a check made out in her name. The dates said two weeks ago.

"Yeah, I know. It's late. Really late, according to Darla. But I had to think about this. I asked around, and yeah, this is what guys do when they knock someone up. At least decent guys do when it's a girl they respect."

Sally's mind whirled with things she could do with $2,400. Even though she'd browsed the second-hand shops, there seemed to be so much stuff that a baby needed.

"Did you keep the same email address?"

Sally nodded.

"Okay, that's good, then. On the first of every month, I've set up an automatic deposit for you from my bank account. The first time you'll need to approve it, but once it's done the first time, then the money will come to you without you having to do anything."

"For how long?"

Daryl shifted uncomfortably. "I dunno. Until the kid is eighteen? How should I know? I've never done this before."

"So, you're giving me $2,800 now, then $400 a month, like forever?"

"Not forever. Sheesh. At some point a kid will be on his own, right?"

"Is this check really good?"

Daryl leveled a gaze at her. "I'm not your mother."

Sally had shared with him some of her problems with her mother.

They sat in silence a minute.

"What do you want out of this? Do you want shared custody?"

"Holy.... No! Not at all. Darla said I need to step up and help pay, even if I did nothing else." Then he added, "Her words, not mine."

"You know that I'll fight you if you try to take this baby from me."

Daryl held up his hands, palms facing Sally. "Whoa. No worries. No way do I want the kid."

Sally carefully folded the check into quarters, then stuffed into the top of her bra. Daryl's eyes followed her every movement. She'd take whatever she could get. It might not last, but then again, Daryl just might keep his word. He differed from the scumbags her mother attracted. Well, sort of.

———

Sally'd been dreading this day for half a year now. Mr. Boyes left a note asking her to stop by his office when her shift was over.

She'd worked for him for almost four years now, first part time, then with full-time hours after she finished high school. Mr. Boyes had been decent to her, as far as bosses went.

During the first trimester of her pregnancy, she'd dragged herself through her shifts, but sometimes she just had to dash to the staff washroom when the nausea grew into an eruption. She feared that the other employees would complain about the stench she left in the women's washroom. If they complained, no word of it reached her ears.

By about the fourth month, her exhaustion lessened, at least somewhat, and the urge to vomit wasn't a part of her every waking moment.

Now she was clumsy. She admitted it. Moving cartons onto the trolley, wheeling them into the aisles and stacking the contents on the shelves was a strain. She tried not to put her hand on her aching back when anyone was around. She switched to shoes that accommodating her swollen feet. She planned out her moves, taking care of how she lifted, and sat rather than stood whenever she could. She was pretty sure no one had noticed these minor changes in her work routine.

But she'd heard of other women being fired for being pregnant, on the excuse that they were not fit for work. Sally could not afford to lose her job.

Mr. Boyes sat behind his desk, playing with a pen. "Come in, Sally. Have a seat." He indicated the empty chair across from him.

Sally concentrated on moving naturally, giving no sign that this lump hanging from her abdomen inconvenienced her in any way.

Boyes cleared his throat. "We'll get right to it. You've worked here for four years and been an excellent employee."

"Thank you." Her thumb began its leisurely sweep up and down the side of the finger next to it.

He tapped his pen up and down on his desktop. "But lately, I'm getting complaints from the other employees."

Sally frowned.

Boyes looked away. "They say you're making them uncomfortable."

What? Sally didn't get it. She tried to be pleasant to everyone, offering a hand when she could, never shirking her duties. She showered before coming to work, didn't have food stains on the front of her clothes, brushed her teeth and didn't fart in public. How could she make people uncomfortable?

"They feel badly about you having to move boxes. They don't think you should lift things in your, um, your state." He nodded toward Sally's midsection.

"Isn't that my business? I'm perfectly capable of doing my job, and I *am* doing it."

"That's the problem. They feel guilty that you are, so rush in to help you. That takes them from their duties. They feel like they have to do their work, plus some of yours, and that's not fair." Before Sally could speak, he continued. "It's because they like you. They see you as a hard-working young woman. But they worry that you'll hurt yourself -

yourself or the baby." He let that sink in. "Maybe this isn't the job for you."

Sally froze. This was it. He was firing her. And for what? For being pregnant? Could he even do that? This was the time for bluntness. "I need this job." And no one was taking it away from her. She'd fight if she had to; she was no stranger to doing difficult things. Her thumb moved faster, pressing harder against her finger.

"I get that. We all rely on our paychecks." Reaching into his drawer, he pulled out a file. "Here's some information for you." The sheet he shoved across the desk said California Pregnancy Disability Leave Law. Boyes had studied the paper already, so summarized it for Sally. "You can take up to four months off work if you are incapacitated during your pregnancy in a way that means you're incapable of doing some essential part of your job."

"But I can't take off now. What about when the baby comes? I'll need some time home with her."

"This disability leave has nothing to do with the twelve weeks of parenting leave you get after the birth. The disability leave is in addition to that." He made direct eye contact. "Your job will be waiting for you when you come back. We don't want to lose you."

"Thanks, but big deal if I can take time off now. That doesn't pay the bills and babies need a lot of stuff."

"This isn't unpaid leave - the State of California will pay you a portion of your salary while you're on disability leave. I already looked into this for you." He named the amount she'd get.

That, with the monthly money from Daryl, would mean she'd bring in a little more than she did while working. Could it be that simple? Could she stay home and rest and get ready for the baby? She'd never considered allowing herself time off. Her imagination conjured up scenarios of having all day to clean the apartment and cook meals, rather than sandwiching everything into those few hours between when she got home from work and falling into bed, exhausted. "So, I just do this?"

Mr. Boyes shook his head. "It's not quite that easy. You need a doctor to say that you can't safely do some aspect of your job here. Lifting produce containers and cases of canned goods is an example." He showed Sally a form that he'd started. It outlined these duties and the approximate weights of some of the items she was required to lift during her eight hours at work.

Sally scanned the sheet, then looked up. "This says that many of our boxes are over 40 pounds." She frowned. "I didn't think they were that heavy."

"Some are, some aren't. But even with the smaller cartons, you shouldn't regularly be lifting anything over 20 pounds at this stage in your pregnancy."

"I need a doctor to sign this?"

Boyes nodded. "I have the paperwork here that you'll need to take." He passed it over. "It, ah, might not hurt if you told the doctor how tired you are, or that your back aches, or other womanly stuff." He couldn't meet her eyes.

Well, she wouldn't be lying if she told the clinic doctor how she felt. That gnawing ache in her back often kept her from much-needed sleep. Still, something nagged at Sally. She hated feeling pushed; she got that enough at home. Maybe it wasn't wise to challenge her employer, but she couldn't help herself. "And if I don't do this?"

"Sally, please don't." He shook his head. "I've had enough complaints from the other employees that I'd have to let you go. None of us want that."

Sally's eyes narrowed and her chin jutted out.

"Sally, we like you. We want you back her working after the baby's born, but we don't want anything to happen to you. Please, for your sake and ours, go apply for this leave."

"I'll think about it." She gathered up the papers he offered her and left the room. Refusing to make eye contact with anyone, she gathered her purse and jacket from her locker and strode out of the building.

Chapter Nineteen

It hurt. Back in high school, Sally was used to being on the outs with her fellow students. Her life differed from theirs drastically. She had no time for the activities they seemed to relish. Their problems seemed so petty compared to all that she had on her plate.

But outside of school, in her job, Sally felt on an equal footing with those around her. When she worked part time in the supermarket as a kid, she never felt looked-down upon by co-workers. Once she started working there full time, she felt comradeship, part of a team. While she might not socialize with them outside of work, she still felt accepted, maybe even friends.

Now, to learn that they'd complained about her, about having to help her and didn't want her around hurt.

Sally's first instinct was to get in their faces, tell them what she thought of them. The baby gave her a slam dunk kick, reminding her of her priorities. She rubbed her stomach. Besides, she simply didn't have the energy for a fight.

The place stank. Although she was positive her olfactory senses were steering her wrong, she detected the underlying odor of urine. Couldn't be. Surely they'd clean it up immediately if there was an accident. But still… tell that to her nose.

Over top of that was the cloying scent of disinfectant. Sure, cleanliness was important, but did they have to shower the place with the stuff?

She never used to be sensitive to smells, but pregnancy did a number on her nose. Stuff she'd never noticed before drove her nuts now. Like meat. She'd always been neutral to meat, but now, the aroma of raw meat had her trotting to the bathroom just as fast as her swollen feet could take her. She avoided the meat department at work the way you would a viper on the loose.

Tugging open the door, Sally exited the clinic, sucking in the fresh air. Fresher, at least, if you ignored the exhaust from the passing bus.

Tired as usual, she felt a weight lifted off her shoulders. It had been easier than she imagined. Sure, the doctor gave her grief about not keeping her last few prenatal appointments, but who could get off work that often? It's not like she was sitting home twiddling her thumbs, looking for things to do and appointments to make. He also told her off for not taking prenatal vitamins, as he'd recommended months earlier. The good part was that he gave her a free sample bottle that should last right up until she birthed the kid.

She put up with his nagging because he immediately signed the papers to get her off work. In fact, he said that she should have come in a month ago, especially considering the demands of her job.

Despite having gained over twenty pounds so far, Sally felt like her feet were floating as she walked down the sidewalk. She didn't have to rush back to work. In fact, she didn't have to go to work period for the next two months before the birth, then for a further twelve weeks after the baby made it into this world. Woo hoo! Never had she felt so free.

"Don't think you're going to sit around here doing nothing," warned Izzy. "I've got no use for laziness. If you're not going to work, there's plenty to do around here."

Sally regarded her mother through half-raised lids from where she lounged on the couch, her swollen feet up on the coffee table.

Sally contemplated how last evening looked, as if she'd video-recorded the whole thing. After leaving the doctor's clinic, she'd walked the several miles to their neighborhood, where she stopped at a grocery store. *Not* the one where she worked. Yep, she'd give her business elsewhere.

Thousands of thoughts swirled through her mind as she walked. All the possibilities. Always numbers conscious, she tallied up how much she spent on bus fare each week getting to and from work. Twenty-five bucks. That was $100 a month!

She'd splurged. Last night they used that $25 for a celebration dinner. It didn't matter that no one but Sally knew where the money came from. Her family took it for granted that food appeared on the table; no one questioned where it came from or how it got there.

While Sally usually avoided the over-priced deli sections

of store, last night she had bought all ready-made foods for her family. No raw meat to touch or smell. No preparation, just open containers and eat. What a treat!

Izzy, thinking she didn't have Sally's attention, repeated herself. "Don't think you're going to sit around here doing nothing. If you're skipping off work, there's plenty to do around here."

"Oh? Like what?" Sally was curious to see if her mother even remembered what it was like to manage a household.

"Well…" Izzy looked around. The place was neat, the dishes done and put away. "Laundry. There's always laundry with four people and those girls think they have to shower every day, sometimes more."

"It's done."

"What about all those boxes and bags you've accumulated? I don't see how you think we have room here for anything else."

"Yeah, I've been meaning to talk to you about that. I'll wait until the girls are here, though." She returned to her textbook, a highlighter in one hand.

"I can't find anything," wailed Laura.

"Me neither," Bethany agreed. "My favorite sweater was right here by my bed and now it's gone."

Sally waited. She knew that when no one raced in to rescue her sisters, they'd eventually come out to complain. And here they come in one, two, three…. Sally moved to the coffee table and picked up the remote. She muted the soap opera her mother had recorded during the week.

"Hey! I'm watching that." Izzy reached for the remote.

Sally held it to her chest and waited for her sisters. "Sit," she told them.

Laura threw herself beside their mother, slouching with her arms crossed. While that pout might have been cute when she was four, at seventeen, it just looked petulant.

Bethany perched on the arm of the couch, rolling her eyes, clearly announcing how all of this was beneath her.

"It's crowded in here," began Sally.

"Yeah, and you keep bringing in more and more stuff." Laura nodded at the boxes in the living room's corner.

"Just where do you think you're going to put this baby?" Ah, Izzy got the crux of the matter.

"That's what we need to talk about. You," she pointed at her mother, "have a bedroom all to yourself. The three of us," she pointed at herself and her sisters, "share the smaller bedroom."

"I need my space. I'm the parent and the bread-winner here."

"True, you're the parent," said Sally. "You're not the sole bread-winner here, though."

Izzy opened her mouth, but Sally didn't let her speak. "I pay for half of everything here." She waited, but no one spoke. "So, I pay for half, yet I have one-third of one room."

"No one asked you to move back in here," said Laura. Then her face creased with worry. She remembered what it was like while Sally was away, the mess of the place, the constant worry over money.

"True," agreed Sally. "We have some choices to make, or I do, but I'd like your input." She had their attention now. Usually Sally made the rules; they were not used to her asking for their opinions. "In a month, this baby will be here. Babies need a lot of stuff and take up room." She pointed to the crib she'd built in the living's corner room by the window. "That's just the start of it."

Bethany did that eye-roll thing again.

Continuing, Sally said, "I organized our bedroom. If everyone puts their things away all the time, it's livable for the three of us."

"Yeah, like *that's* ever going to happen with a slob like Bethany around," said Laura.

"Me? You're worse." Bethany was willing to get into it.

Sally held up her hand. "I said *if.* That's a choice you'll have to make. The baby and I need room. This will mean that four of us share that bedroom. If we divide the room up, that means the baby and I take up half of the room."

"What! That's not fair! What am I supposed to do with all of my stuff?" Both girls were now on the same side.

"That's option A," said Sally. "Option B is that I continue to share a room with you two, but the baby takes up a portion of this living room."

Her mother and sisters scanned the room they were in. To one side was the desk that held the laptop. There was a couch and coffee table pointed at the television, the couch flanked by small end tables. In the L shape of the room was a kitchen table with six chairs. An old beanbag chair occupied the intervening space. Or it used to. Now bags and boxes of baby paraphernalia flanked it. The crib took up most of the space. Sally hadn't yet put together the shelving unit that would hold the tiny clothes, blankets, and diapers.

"Babies cry." Bethany said.

"Yes. Sometimes in the night."

"How are we supposed to get any sleep? I have exams coming up and need my rest," Laura said.

"That brings us to option C." Sally paused. "I move out and get my own place."

Silence.

"That would mean it's back to just two of us in the bedroom," said Bethany. "More room, and no one nagging us to clean up."

Maybe they'd spoiled her too much, thought Sally. The kid could never see past herself.

Izzy, though, had a moment of clarity when reality sunk in. As much as their mother tried to pretend certain things were so deep inside, she felt a kernel of truth, no matter how hard she tried to push it back down. Sally could tell by her mother's eyes that the fleeting thoughts of what life was like without Sally here to manage things.

Laura also had an inkling, at least on the financial side of things. "But you'd still pay for stuff around here, right?"

Sally shook her head. "No, if I have my own place, it would take all of my income to support myself and my baby."

Only Bethany didn't get those ramifications. She thought a second, then asked Sally, "But you'd still come back to cook lasagna sometimes, wouldn't you? I *love* your lasagna."

Sally smiled and nodded. Her throat felt too full to speak. She'd known that her family valued her for what she did for them. Still, confirmation of that hurt. These people didn't have one comment about what might be best for *Sally*, only for themselves.

Had she contributed to these people being so self-centered? Or maybe that was just the way folks were. She straightened. It was time to do the same for herself. After all, there was no one else to look out for her.

Gathering up her purse, she moved toward the door. "I've changed my mind. Forget these options. The decision involves me, and I'll make it on my own." Then she was gone.

Chapter Twenty

Duty. Love. Responsibility. A life.

Sally pondered all these things. She was sick of it.

The streetlights created puddles of light, then she'd step into the shadows until the next, unbroken light. One hand supported her bulging belly, mindful of where she put her feet on the crumbling sidewalk.

Yes, she had a duty to her family. She'd done that.

Yes, she was sure they loved her, in their own fashion. At least she was pretty sure of that.

Was this to be her life? Should she forever be enslaved to her mother and sisters? How would they manage without her?

Her other hand rubbed a spot on her stomach, feeling the outline of a little foot pushing. Or was it a fist? What of this new life she cradled? What did she owe it? *More* than she owed Izzy and the girls?

She was in a different part of town now. It was obvious where the change started - no more broken streetlights, no more trash in the gutters, no upside-down shopping carts, with wheels moving in the breeze. Was it possible that it even smelled better?

Comfort Inn. Sally stopped and stared at the sign. Comfort was exactly what she needed. When had she last felt comfort of any kind? Maybe she'd had it for a while with Daryl.

Of their own accord, her feet turned her up the driveway of the hotel. She'd never stayed in one before. The sign said $99. That was a lot for a room.

Sally did a mental tally of what was in her bank account. Since learning to manage her mother's finances, her skills with numbers and budgets grew until she could almost predict what her bank balance would be at any time of the month. Could she splurge and spend a hundred bucks on a night here? A night of indulgence, just for herself?

Yes, she mostly had everything she'd need for the baby, at least according to the books she'd studied. Still, a hundred bucks was a hundred bucks.

"For how many nights, please?" The woman behind the desk smiled a welcome, as if a pregnant lady walking in off the streets without a suitcase was a common occurrence.

"One, please." Shoot. Do I pay now or when I leave? She hated looking foolish.

The woman helped her out. "I'll need a credit card impression, please."

"Do you want me to pay now or in the morning?"

"Up to you, dearie, but we need a credit card on file if you're not paying in full now."

Sally handed over her Visa. She reminded herself that this would help build up her points, so it wouldn't be a total indulgence.

"If you're missing any toiletries or snacks, we have an

area over there where you can purchase what you need." She pointed to an alcove, then to a doorway across the hall. "Breakfast is continental style and open from seven to eleven tomorrow morning. Just help yourself." She handed Sally a folder containing her room key and a card with the internet password.

What luxury! A thick carpet, prints on the walls, a fifty-inch television with a remote, heavy drapes that did a decent job of blocking out the pools of light coming from the parking lot below. She let her body flop backwards onto the bed. A king-sized bed, and all to herself.

A long counter with two drawers, a desk area with a chair, then two armchairs bordering a round table. Sally pulled open every drawer and cupboard. She found a tiny fridge - empty, but still cool. Above it sat a microwave.

There was a closet if she'd had anything to hang up, with a full-length mirror beside it. After one quick glance, Sally averted her eyes. Pregnancy was not pretty. How many times had Izzy told her that?

Last, she approached a door. Wow! She had not expected to have her own bathroom, thought she'd have to share one with other hotel guests, like in a dormitory. Look at all the white towels, neatly folded. And those were just the hand towels. There were four, count 'em - four, bath towels as well. On the bathroom counter was a selection of tiny bottles containing shampoo, conditioner, hand lotion, a sewing kit, and a shoe shining cloth. Wow, and all for her.

She turned on every light. Picking up the remote, she placed all four pillows under her head and channel surfed. When had she last been in control of a remote? Like, never.

And all these pillows. Ah, she could get used to this life. How decadent.

Persistent kicking snagged her attention. She needed to pay attention to this little life-to-be. She placed both palms on her abdomen and stroked. "Wait, wee one. Just wait until you can see a place like this. I promise to bring you here one day." In the meantime, though, she needed to feed herself. A few blocks away, Sally had spied the parking lot of a Walmart.

Hooking a shopping basket into the crook of her elbow, Sally browsed. She found a t-shirt and sweatpants that would be good for sleepwear, plus she could use them afterwards. She found a travel-sized toothbrush and toothpaste kit for a dollar. A miniature deodorant stick and a comb completed her purchases on that side of the store. Wait, what was that? A bath bomb. She'd heard of them, but never used one. Rose, lilac, chamomile, and cherry. Rose sounded the most relaxing of the fragrances. The round, chalky ball went into her shopping basket.

In the grocery section, Sally found a microwavable meal that would do for supper. The deli area had plastic cutlery.

As she lined up to pay, all sorts of tempting goodies presented themselves, designed to catch the eye of the impulse shopper. Impulsive, Sally was not. But still.... A package of microwave popcorn somehow found its way into her basket.

Checking out, her purchases came to just over twenty dollars. A lot to spend on one person for one night, but she was on a roll. She could afford it; never would she be like Izzy and spend to make herself feel good when she didn't have the cash to spare. She'd spent the last seven years putting everyone else first. Tonight was her night.

A bath in an already-clean tub, with the perfumed fragrance of her bath bomb. When the water started to cool off, she simply added more hot water. No one pounding on the door saying they needed to pee. No one complaining that they were hungry and couldn't find anything to eat. With her stomach satiated from her microwaved dinner, she relaxed fully into her bath. She even used a towel for nothing but cradling her head against the shiny, white porcelain of the tub. No one to please but herself. Ah, this was the life.

After her toes and fingertips were sufficiently pruney, Sally toweled off, and dressed in her new duds. Warm and comfy, she popped a bag of popcorn into the microwave. Never had she had popcorn all to herself. What a treat.

Arranging all the pillows just so around her back, Sally settled back to enjoy herself. Nothing on TV quite grabbed her attention. Her mind worried about the problem of their living arrangements. She went over and over her options, the ones she had laid out for her mother and sisters.

Before tonight, she would have landed on choice A or B. But this evening, the experience of being on her own, responsible only for herself, changed things.

Reaching for her phone, Sally did some research on apartments. There wasn't a lot in the price range she was willing to consider. Some were too far from her job, necessitating a lengthy bus ride with transfers. Some were in questionable buildings, not that Sally was that picky. But she knew some places would be too unsafe for a growing baby.

There was one vacancy right in her mother's apartment building, a one-bedroom apartment, on the ground floor.

Sally put down her phone and closed her eyes. What would it be like living so close to her family? She knew the building and the area well, so that was a plus. She could easily get to work. If she needed help, her mom and sisters would be nearby and able to get there quickly.

But would they? And would the proximity mean that they'd still expect Sally to do all the things she currently did for them?

She bookmarked the place and sent out a tentative query to their building's manager.

Breakfast was leisurely. Dawdling over her selections of muffins, bagels, cereals, Belgian waffles, juices, fresh fruits, and coffee, Sally debated what she'd say to her mom and sisters when she got home.

A ping from her phone indicated an incoming email. The landlady, replying to Sally's query about the one-bedroom apartment.

Izzy painted the landlady as an ogre out to get them. But over the last half-dozen years, Sally had gotten to know her. While no saint, the women wasn't that bad. Her threats stemmed from frustrations over Izzy not paying the rent. Under Sally's hands, they'd never been late with the rent check and the woman had warmed considerably to Sally's family.

But the news in the email was not good. Yes, the apartment was still open and yes, she'd willingly rent it to Sally. The bad news was that the price tag was much higher than the $450 a month the advertisement stated. The management company that ran the building required a year's lease.

That was no problem. But they needed the first month's rent, the last month's rent, *plus* a damage deposit equivalent to an additional month's rent. Instead of needing to come up with $450 to get the place, Sally somehow had to find the impossible sum of $1350. The cinnamon bun she'd just enjoyed turned sour in her stomach.

So much for that idea. Yeah, she had some cash in her savings account, but who knew how much she'd need for this baby? She wouldn't be back at work for another four months.

Gathering up her used plates and utensils, Sally took her tray to the counter, depositing her waste in the trash can. Returning to her room, she didn't regard her sanctuary with as much delight as she did last night. She'd opened the drapes before heading down for breakfast, and the harsh sunlight pointed out things she'd overlooked the night before. Now the stains on the carpet stood out in stark relief. The path around the bed and toward the bathroom worn from countless feet. The artwork screwed to the wall hadn't been swapped out in decades. The air conditioner started up with a rattle as fan blades scraped against something it ought not to be touching.

Her phone gave a beep that meant a text message had arrived. It was from Daryl. He'd typed, "Can we meet? It's important."

Just what she needed. Something more to cope with. Well, this would be on her terms. She gave him the address of her hotel, saying she'd meet him in the eating area in half an hour.

Daryl looked everywhere but at Sally's burgeoning middle section. His eyes slid by hers as well.

"Here's the thing," he said. "I lost my job."

Oh, no. This could not be good.

"It's tough. I've been looking, but nothing's cropped up yet." Slowly, he spun his coffee cup in a circle, regarding the dark liquid with intense interest. "I have some savings, you know, but it won't last forever." He gave a quick glance at Sally's face. "I know what I said about the kid," he gave a nod toward their baby growing in Sally's belly. "But at the time I didn't know I'd be out of a job. I can continue to pay you while you're pregnant and until you go back to work." Just to make sure she was clear about this, he explained, "That's for four more months."

"What happened to your promise of until the kid is 18? *Our* kid?"

He shrugged. "Stuff happens, you know?" There was a slight reddening to his cheeks. "Besides, my girlfriend says it's not fair. She's ticked that I give you four hundred a month - says it's money we could be doing things with."

Ah, now that made sense.

"What would your sister say?"

Another shrug. "It's not her life. And she doesn't have to know."

"I could fight you on this."

"Yeah. But you wouldn't." Then, with less confidence, "Would you?"

"I haven't decided."

His cocky grin was back, the one that had so appealed to her in the beginning. "I know you."

True. That was the problem.

Chapter Twenty-One

Sally's elation at her holiday night in the hotel withered, dried up and blew away in the breeze that smacked her in the face as she trudged back home.

With her head down, she didn't notice the man until she was almost beside him. What was this guy doing in front of their apartment door? And with boxes and a suitcase?

Using his knuckles, he rapped on the door. "Izzy? Come on, open up."

Keys in hand, Sally glared at the man. How did he know Izzy?

The door opened and Izzy's smiling visage appeared. "Robert! Come in, come in. We've been waiting for you." She stood aside to let him in, then wrapped her arms around his neck. "Sally, bring in those boxes, would you?" To Robert, "Bring your things into my room. Right this way."

Robert pulled his suitcase down the short hall. It listed to one side, and he had to keep correcting its path since part of one wheel was broken off. "What's to eat? I'm starved."

"Sally's been out gallivanting about, but now that she's home, she'll get some food going for us."

Robert stopped and turned. He looked Sally up and down. "So that's your gal, eh? And she's a cook. Good to know. I can boil wieners but that's about it." He gave Sally a friendly smile. "Looking forward to sampling your cooking." He removed one arm from Izzy's shoulders and pointed at Sally's belly. "How does she cook around that thing?" He laughed at his joke, Izzy joining in. Noticing that Sally was following with one of his boxes, he directed her. "No, those go in the living room."

After dumping his suitcase on the bed, Robert and Izzy returned to the living room, Izzy settled in his lap on the couch. "What's all that stuff?" Robert asked, pointing at the crib and boxes neatly stacked up against one wall in the living room.

"That's Sally's baby stuff."

"I'm going to need that space for my flat screen TV. We can't watch on that piddly thing." He waved his hand toward Izzy's television. "And I need room for my Play Station stuff."

"Don't worry," Izzy assured him. "It'll be out of there."

Later, after she'd cleared away the remains of their supper, Sally grabbed her mother's arm and pulled her into the kitchen. "Why'd you bring him here?" They were short on space as it was. "And where am I supposed to store my stuff for the baby?"

"In your own place." Izzy's gaze penetrated that of her oldest daughter. "When you left here yesterday, I knew that you'd be abandoning us. I know you think I'm an airhead." She stifled Sally's attempt at a protest. "I'm well aware my salary alone can't carry this place. With you running off, I need someone to help with the rent. Robert's been hanging around me for a while, so it took little encouragement for him to beg to move in here."

"But I don't have a place," Sally started to say. It was no use. Izzy had returned to her perch on Robert's lap.

Two phone calls. "Mrs. Higgins, this is Sally Ramirez. Is that apartment still available?" It was. "I'll take it."

The next was to Daryl. "I've decided. I don't trust you. Since you reneged on supporting your child until it's eighteen, we have a problem. I could sue you for child support. That'd be fair, but it'd be a hassle for both of us. So, here's what we're going to do…"

Daryl agreed with reluctance, after first trying to bully his way out of this. But he didn't know her as well as he thought he did. Or maybe the Sally he thought he knew had morphed into something too big for him to handle.

In less than an hour, Daryl <u>slid</u> into the booth across from Sally at McDonald's. First, he slid across the table a paper torn from a writing pad. It said,

I, Daryl Brown, revoke any rights I have to the baby that Sally Ramirez is carrying.

Below the words, he'd scrawled his name and today's date.

"There," he said. "Word for word what you said you wanted."

Sally folded the page evenly into quarters and slid it into a side compartment of her purse. "That's the first part."

He fished his wallet out of his pants. "You know this pretty much cleans me out, don't you?"

As if Sally cared. She waited.

With a sigh, he opened his wallet and counted out 15 hundred-dollar bills.

"That's not all of it."

"Geez, Sally, you're killing me."

She gave a pointed glance at her midsection wedged into the table, then at Daryl.

"All right." Digging two fifties out of his wallet, he passed them over. "We square now?"

Sally counted the money, folding it in half, then placing it in her wallet. "Not quite. You have something that belongs to me."

"Like what?"

"My table. The one I carried home and restored. And the chairs that go with it."

"That thing? You can have it. Janie thinks it's ugly and wants it out of there. She'll be happy to see it go."

"Who's Janie?"

"My girlfriend."

"Oh." It hadn't taken him long to replace her. "You need to bring the table and chairs to my place."

"Okay. I'll do that this afternoon." He'd get a buddy with a truck to help. "*Now* we're square?" How had she never noticed that whine that crept into Daryl's tone?

"For now." Best to not close all doors. Without another glance at the father of her baby, the man she maybe once thought she loved, she leveraged herself out of the booth, trying not to groan with the effort, and left the building.

After giving the damage deposit, plus two months' rent to the landlady, Sally signed the lease papers, painstakingly reading the fine print, and received the keys to the apartment. *Her* apartment, the first one that she could call all her own. Well, at least for another month until her daughter made her entrance into this world and joined her. She rubbed her hand over her belly, soothing the gently kicking baby within. Exercise time.

The apartment had supposedly been cleaned, yet Sally could see areas she'd need to go over again. She wondered if she could convince Daryl to rent a carpet cleaner and bring it over when he came with her table. But how would she get it back?

The problem with an unfurnished place was that it was, well, unfurnished. She'd have a table and four chairs, but that was it.

Since she'd paid for some of the bedding used in Izzy's place, Sally had no problem with bringing what she needed with her. But she needed a bed to put it on. With her awkward lump of a stomach, sleeping on the floor was out of the question. Or, if she did, there was little chance of being able to hoist herself up off the floor again.

If she could locate a bed and a couch, maybe she could make Daryl use his truck to pick them up for her. The chances of that were less if his Janie was along. Still, Sally bet she knew more about getting Daryl to bend to her will than did this Janie.

For now, though, she could move some of the smaller stuff down.

"What's going on here?" Robert's voice could be heard in the apartment across the hall. "What's a pregnant lady doing trying to carry this stuff?"

Sally looked at him. He'd not said anything when Izzy told her to bring his box in from the hallway the day before.

"Laura! Bethany!" He roared their names. With slow steps, the girls came out of their room.

Seeing Sally, Laura groaned. "Is she moving back in?"

"I've never moved out."

"We were just talking about how we're going to divide up our bedroom," added Bethany. "There'll be lots more room without you and the baby stuff."

"Girls," ordered Robert. "Take that box from your sister and carry it for her." To Sally, "Where are ya taking it, love?"

Sally's nose wrinkled at the endearment, but he didn't seem to mean it in a slimy way. It was just a question. "I've rented an apartment two floors down."

"And you want all this stuff moved there?" Robert pointed at the crib and stacked boxes.

Sally nodded.

"Let's get to it, girls." As Sally bent for a box, he said, "Not you. You shouldn't be lifting. I meant your sisters. We'll have you moved and set up in no time." He hefted three boxes at once, then raised his booming voice again. "Izzy! Your daughter's here for her things. The girls and I will move the boxes while you pack up her clothes." He went out the door and down the hallway without a doubt in his mind that they would follow his orders. "Lead the way, love." Sally did as told.

After placing their loads on the floor of Sally's new place, Robert looked around. "Not a bad size but could use some work." He checked around the corner. "Are you happy with the condition of this carpet?"

Sally shook her head.

"Is there someplace around here where we could rent a rug shampooer?"

"Yeah." The supermarket where she worked had them.

"Well, let's go get it." He instructed Laura and Bethany to move down the rest of Sally's things and organize them.

"How?" Bethany asked.

Looking around, Robert got her point. "Do you have any furniture, girl?"

Again, Sally shook her head.

"Cripes. What was Izzy thinking? Can't have a pregnant girlie sitting on the floor. Come on. We'll see what we can find for you."

Sally's feet didn't move.

"Come on. I have to be at work by three, so we only have a couple of hours to buy your stuff and get it back here. Hop in my truck."

Izzy appeared in the doorway and caught just the last statement Robert made. As she made to leave with him, he stopped her. "No, I'll take your girl to get some furniture. You stay here and organize this place, make it nice for her."

It took three second-hand shops until it satisfied Robert that they'd found the best things they could for the price Sally was willing to pay. They even found a mattress still in its original plastic wrapping. "You know you're not getting cooties that way," explained Robert. Sally picked up a decent leather couch and a dresser. While she searched through the mismatched plates and cutlery, pots and pans, Robert instructed the store manager to throw in the matching swivel rocking chair and paid for it himself. He haggled until the store agreed to deliver their purchases and within the next two hours. "Are we good to go, girlie?"

Sally nodded.

"Don't talk much, do ya? Never mind, we'll get along fine anyway. Now hop in my truck and we'll go get that carpet cleaner."

As Robert followed Sally's directions, pulling into the supermarket, he realized where they were. "Crikey. You have no food. You'll need to stock up. You go do your shopping while I see about renting this machine." When she hesitated, he said, "My treat. Today's groceries are on me. It's a big day when you get your own place."

Was this guy for real? Izzy had never had a boyfriend like this. He seemed, well, nice. That was not Izzy's usual type.

Robert wouldn't let Sally carry in any of the groceries she'd bought. *He'd* bought. Never had someone done so much for her. When she first came to the check-out counter with her shopping cart of groceries, Robert sent her back for more, saying she needed to stock up on staples. She was eating for two; how was she supposed to cook without the basics?

Bossy Robert insisted Sally stand back and direct her sisters on where to put the groceries, but only after they'd first wiped out the cupboards. This chore was a first for both Laura and Bethany. Were they happy about it? Nope. But neither was willing to defy Robert. There was something about him…

Izzy didn't evade his orders, either. Her job was to organize Sally's bedroom. The store's delivery guys had arrived by then, so Izzy made up the bed and folded clothing into the dresser. On Robert's suggestion, she even took hangers from her own closet to use in Sally's.

"Damn, girl." Robert looked around. "We didn't get you anything to eat on."

"That's okay. I have a table and chairs coming this afternoon."

"Good girl." He felt the newly shampooed carpet. "Mostly dry. It'll be good by tonight. I'd better get this rental thing back to the store." He asked for Sally's mobile phone number. After tapping on his own, Sally's beeped. "There. Now you have my number. Text me if there's anything you need. I gotta get this thing back before I go to work." Then he left.

All three girls looked at their mother. Where did she find this guy?

"See what a difference a man makes?" said Izzy. "He gets things done for you. He goes to work. He brings in money." She looked at all three of her daughters. "Aren't you glad I hooked up with him?"

Izzy suggested that since they'd done all this work for Sally, it was only fair that she cook them supper.

With her larder fuller than ever in her life, Sally happily obliged.

"You'll still cook for us, right?" Bethany wanted to know.

"Maybe sometimes, but I don't live there anymore." Sally needed to establish some boundaries now. "You, Laura and Mom could take turns cooking."

All three looked at her like she'd lost her mind.

"I'll be busy with the baby and doing my own stuff here," Sally explained.

"But you still need to eat," said Bethany. "You could make enough for all of us."

"Nope." Sally would not go there. "It'll be like when I moved out before. You're on your own."

Laura was quiet while Sally cleared the table. She stayed behind when Bethany left to hang out with her friends and Izzy went upstairs to watch television. "Makes no sense that you have no TV, girl," she complained. Televisions cost money, as did the cable fees. Sally had a laptop, and that was enough for her.

Laura even ran water in the sink and started washing the dishes. A first, thought Sally.

It took a while before Laura voiced her concerns, but once she started, it spilled out. "You know what happened to us the last time you moved out."

Sally nodded.

"Everything went to shit. The place was a mess. We had nothing but junk food until the money ran out and the bills weren't paid."

"It'll be better now. We cut down on Mom's spending money so there is more cash for expenses, and now Robert will pay some of the rent."

The girls looked at each other. That had been the idea when Mom brought other men home to live with them, but rarely had it worked out. Most of them freeloaded or offered cash only from time to time and acted like they were doing them a big favor when they did.

"Robert seems different," said Sally. "Maybe this time it really will be different."

"Mom says it will be," added Laura, but she'd seen this scenario often enough to be skeptical. "At least he doesn't touch me." She washed another plate. "Or even look like a creep at Bethany or me."

"Don't let him do anything to you. If he tries it, come down here to me." Now why had she made that offer?

"I don't get that vibe from him. But Sally, when I had to pay the bills, I made a mess of it."

"So did I when I first started, but you'll get the hang of it."

"It takes so much time. And how am I supposed to look after the place while I'm going to school? I need to get good grades so that I can get out of here and make a life for myself. I'm *not* getting trapped here like Mom and…" She stopped herself in time, but Sally knew what she'd been going to say. Once upon a time Sally, too, had dreams of getting out of here, of bettering herself. Maybe it wasn't too late. She glanced down at her belly.

Chapter Twenty-Two

"Please, please, please?" Bethany begged, making the doe-eyed look she'd perfected. "I *hate* Laura's food and I'm sick of pizza."

Sally caved. Yeah, Bethany, the master manipulator, was working it, and she won. Sally brought all the ingredients and cooked supper for her family, making enough that they could reheat the leftovers tomorrow.

Sally stood at the sink washing the supper dishes when her water broke.

"Ew, gross!" Bethany pointed. "Look, she peed her pants." She partially hid her giggles behind her hand.

Laura noticed. "*I'm* not cleaning that up."

Izzy's eyes met Sally's. She knew what this meant. For a few seconds, something flickered. Sympathy? Understanding? Then it went away. "Better wipe that up before it dries and stains." Her gaze returned to the television.

On her knees cleaning up the mess, the first pain struck. Oh! No one said it would hurt this much. Doubled over, she wrapped her arms around her stomach. As the steel band loosened, Sally lifted her head and let out a breath. From the couch, Laura watched her sister with frightened eyes. When their glances met, Laura quickly averted her eyes, pretended fascination with a rerun of *Grey's Anatomy*.

Using the counter for support, Sally dragged herself to her feet. Clutching her gut, she walked toward the desk where she left her purse, when another convulsing pain surged. Early labor pains were supposed to be ten minutes apart at least, weren't they?

Desperately, she looked at her mother. Izzy, watching her through narrowed eyes, said, "You made your bed, now lie in it."

Cradling her gut, Sally hunched over, teeth clenched, breathing through the sides of her mouth. When she could move again, she pulled her cell phone from her purse, did a quick search, then dialled an Uber number.

Robert was at work. If he'd been there, would he have offered to drive her to the hospital? Gone with her? Didn't matter; she was fine on her own. Always had been.

Just down two flights of stairs, not far. For first births, labor started gradually, at least that's what the books said. No problem; lots of time.

In the stairwell between the first and second floors, the next pain struck, sharp and fast. In the time it took her to suck in a breath, grasp the handrail with both hands and lower her bottom to the stair tread, it was over. Not fun, but tolerable.

Every time Sally walked into the sanctity of her apartment, her bowed shoulders relaxed. Peace. Quiet. Everything in its place.

The Uber would be there within fifteen minutes. Time to freshen up a bit and make sure that everything was ready for when she brought the baby home.

The Uber driver insisted she wait in his car until he returned with a wheelchair. Helping Sally into it, he pushed her through the hospital doors. He insisted that the nurse wait while he returned to the car for Sally's small valise. The kindness of strangers.

"Will your partner be returning once he's parked his car?"

"Oh, he's not my partner," Sally explained to the nurse. "He's an Uber driver."

"Should we be expecting anyone with you?"

Sally shook her head.

As the nurse pushed Sally's chair past the admitting desk, Sally noticed a gorgeous cluster of flowers. Long, elegant stems. Pure white blossoms, with a vivid red stripe. Such perfection. "Stop. Please." She raised her hand toward the floral arrangement. "What are those?"

With barely a glance, the nurse replied, "Lilies."

What was it that the books said about first babies coming slowly? Sally's suitcase held several books, ones she hoped would keep her attention riveted on them and not on her convulsing midsection. But she barely made it through the first chapter when her life spun out of control. All the breathing patterns in the world couldn't contain this pain. Pant through it. Sure. Count. Blow out. Right. Whoever wrote those things had never been in this situation, one where a voracious creature took over your insides, determined to split them apart to make its way into the world.

All her warm, fuzzy feelings toward this baby flew out the window, along with her stoicism and control and plans. She was tough. She could do it. Not!

By the time the epidural took effect, she was boneless, except for that tightening band of steel around her abdomen. Never had she known such utter exhaustion and such utter terror.

Finally, as the sedative took over, she lay there, letting the medical people and her body do to her what they would. Funny, laying there, letting others do things to her body, was sort of what got her into this mess in the first place.

She drifted as the action took place around her - nurses bustling about, sheets drenched in bright red being whisked away, the doctor calling orders. She shut her eyes against the overly bright light centered over her narrow, cold, hard gurney.

A nurse rubbed Sally's hand between her own. "Ms. Ramirez, Ms. Ramirez." Someone else brushed her cheeks, not that gently. An urgent voice called, "Sally. Sally, open your eyes."

Why couldn't they let her sleep. She'd been through so much. Now that the pain subsided, she needed to sleep. Didn't they know that soon she'd have a baby to look after? She'd be a single mom. She needed her rest now.

A weight plunked on her stomach. No, not there. Be careful of my baby. Don't push there.

"Sally, your baby's here. Sally, wake up and see your daughter. She's beautiful."

What? Here? When did that happen? Sally raised her head just an inch. Sure enough, there was a blanket-swaddled bundle on top of her. Not in her. Not anymore. "My baby?"

"Yes, you have a beautiful little girl. Do you have a name for her?"

"Lily. She's my Lily."

Hands guided Sally's to the wrapped bundle. But Sally's neck could not hold up her head any longer. As her skull flopped back onto the pillow, her arms fell away as well, and she sunk into blackness.

The night passed in a blur of fitful sleep interspersed with nurses bringing in the baby for feedings. Couldn't they just let her sleep?

Early, too early, that dratted nurse returned, cheerfully opening the curtains with one hand, the other cradling the baby. The shrieking baby. "Goodness, but she's a hungry one, isn't she?"

Obviously. Another creature with demanding needs. Wasn't her life already full enough with people like that?

Pulling the sheets over her head did no good. The nurse laughed and yanked them down, cranking the bed up until Sally was in a sitting position. "Just time for a quick feed before you're discharged."

Released? "You mean I'm going home now?"

"Soon. You have time to give this young lady some milk and change her diaper before your discharge papers are ready. Is someone coming to pick you up?"

Good question. Mom would be getting ready for work now and wouldn't want to be bothered stopping by the hospital. Besides, it would make her late for work. She couldn't afford to be docked pay.

She hated to spend the money on another Uber, but she was just not up to figuring out which busses she'd need to get home. Maybe dare she try it? Robert had given her his number, saying to call if she needed anything.

He came. In fact, Robert was there before the nurse finished helping Sally pack up her things. "Your mom is sorry she couldn't be here," he said.

Right.

Robert pulled back the blanket to peek at the infant on Sally's lap. "Beautiful. Izzy will be so pleased to be a grandma."

Did he know her mother at all? Whatever.

Robert let her carry nothing but Lily, wrapping an arm around her waist as he walked her to her apartment. "Can't have the little mother tripping with this precious bundle." He settled her into the rocking chair he'd purchased and put her suitcase in the bedroom. "All right then, girlie?" He turned to go. "We're right upstairs if you need anything. You just call and one of us will be right down."

Right. How could he live with Izzy, Laura and Bethany and say such things? Still, Izzy was right - a man came in handy.

The day both dragged and flew by, with most of Sally's time spent dozing in the rocking chair, Lily cradled in her arms. Not that Sally ached to hold her child; the kid grizzled when alone in her crib and Sally got more rest if she did whatever she could to keep the kid quiet.

Just how many times a day did a baby need to eat? *This* baby seemed to think it was her right to suck on Sally's tit at least every hour. She didn't care that Sally's breasts hurt; the nipples sore from the incessant tugging. Good thing the kid didn't come with teeth. Just when did kids get teeth? She'd definitely quit nursing before then.

Why did this kid pee so often? And the other - she spewed crap half-way up her back the last time. Half the package of diapers Sally'd bought was already soiled and in the garbage. At this rate, she'd need to buy more tomorrow. How was she supposed to go to the store with a baby?

Finally, a few hours of peace while Lily slept. Maybe crying exhausted the kid, and she'd sleep for a civilized amount of time.

Sally was alone, having moved the crib into the living room. How had she ever felt sorry for herself for being alone? Now, she relished the solitude of being in her bedroom by herself. How could a being less than two feet long demand so much time and energy?

How did other people cope with this? Maybe when there were two people sharing the chores, it was easier. But Sally was alone. She'd managed all sorts of things on her own, all her life. And succeeded, too.

This, though, this felt too much. Yet another person expecting her to do everything.

Chapter Twenty-Three

A little before noon, Robert rapped on the door. "I just wanted to check that you and the wee one were doing all right," he explained.

Sally lied. "We're fine."

Robert's narrowed eyes showed skepticism. "Your mom is sorry that she can't come help you out. She thinks she's coming down with the sniffles and fears infecting the baby."

Right.

Robert continued. "I tried to send Laura down, but she disappeared. Me thinks girl is afraid of the baby."

Afraid? Afraid of getting trapped into helping.

"Anything you need, girlie? I'm not much with babies myself, but do you need any food or stuff?"

Sally returned with the half-empty case of infant diapers. "She's going through these fast. If you could bring some more, that would really help."

Robert took a picture of the package, so he'd get the right thing. "Be back in half an hour."

He did better than that. When he returned, he had two packages of diapers, plus an assortment of take-away food from the deli.

"Thanks, but I don't have enough cash on me to repay you."

"Oh, girlie, think nothing of it. My gift. I can't help with the baby, but I can fetch things for you." He checked out his shoes, then looked back at Sally. "I'm sure your mom will be better in another day, then she'll be here to help you out."

Sally met his gaze but said nothing.

"Don't you have any girlfriends who could come help you?"

Sally shook her head. Girlfriends? Who had time to make friends? Besides, most people made friends in high school, then stuck with those buds over the years. Sally had no friends in school; there was never time for stuff like that.

That's okay. She was enough for herself; always had been, always would be. Although it might be nice to have a man like Robert around. He had his uses.

Laying on her mattress, the gift from Robert, Sally nestled the baby at her breast. Cradling her precious child, she vowed to always protect her, to give her the life she deserves.

Tears streaked her face, soaking her pillow. Feeling sorry for herself was wasted energy, energy she didn't have to spare. Things would be different for Lily; she would make it so.

Three months dragged on and flew by. Life at home with a baby was, well, not really a life. Instead of fulfilling days as a mother, tedium and impatience dominated the waking hours.

While work in a supermarket was not exactly stimulating, being out with otherpeople was. Sally quickly dove back into the routine, almost as if she'd never been away. Except for the added chore of dropping Lily off at the Infant Care Center before work and picking her up afterwards. It made the day long.

But, once home, she had only herself to feed. No Laura or Bethany to grouse about when supper would be ready. Yeah, the baby's bottles were a pain to prepare, but now that they'd worked out a system of propping up the bottle, the kid pretty much fed herself.

And Sally had her body back. Lily had hijacked it for nine whole months, then came that nursing thing. At first, breastfeeding the kid seemed like the easiest thing. But good lord, would she never have her body back to herself? Bottles provided some needed distance, plus it worked better at the daycare. Besides, who wanted to go around with leaking boobs? Or worse, drooping boobs. Would they never go back to their regular shape if they were used as a feed sack for a year? Nope, not gonna risk that.

Fall rolled around again and with it, the start of classes. Another course in the accounting program began. This time, it would work.

Education was the key - the way out of the life that Izzy had made for herself and her daughters. With a decent education, Sally would make more money. She'd have a career, not just a job. She'd be somebody.

The night school course started next week. God, the exhaustion. How had she done this before? Must have been younger because at that time she'd worked full time and looked after her mom and her sisters, or Daryl. But there'd be time to sleep later. This certification would build a better life for herself and her daughter.

Laura was to babysit. This was in exchange for cash, as well as cooking dinner for the family, plus cleaning their bathroom. Not sure the bargain was fair, but it was all Sally had to work with.

As the time drew close for Sally to leave if she was to get to class on time, there was no Laura. Izzy and Bethany were not home either, so there wasn't even their reluctant backup.

With no other solution, Sally bundled up the sleeping baby and took her to the night class. Apologizing to the instructor, explaining that her sitter never showed up, but that Lily is such a good baby, she will be quiet. They'll never know that she is there.

Choosing a seat at the back of the room, Sally settled in, the sleeping Lily angelic in her car seat.

Then Lily woke up with a wail. Normally a contented baby, she shrieked, arching her back as if in pain. Sally grabbed Lily and took her out into the hallway, but none of the usual things soothed the baby. Even with the classroom door shut, the sounds reverberated throughout the hallway. Other classroom doors opened with people sticking their heads out to see what was the matter.

Sally missed most of the class because of Lily's fussiness. Afterword, the instructor asked to speak to her. Sally apologized, but the instructor said this must not happen ever again. Sally agreed.

The next week, Laura was to babysit in exchange for Sally cleaning their apartment and cooking meals every day that week. Laura *forgot* last week, she said. Plus, Mom would be home.

Sally knew from experience that her mother was unreliable, as unreliable as Laura. So, she researched ways to keep her baby quiet. She read about Benadryl. Loathe to give anything like that to her little girl, but she couldn't risk Lily crying through another class.

She was right. Her mother did not appear to babysit, and Laura was nowhere to be found.

Taking a guess at an appropriate dose of Benadryl for a three-month-old baby, Sally placed the dropper of liquid along the inside of Lily's cheek and squirted. It worked. Lily slept like a cherub for the whole lecture.

After the class, Sally tried to awaken Lily to nurse her. The child refused to be roused.

Sally luxuriated in getting a full night's sleep. She stretched and smiled. This was how sleep was supposed to be. Well, the bottle was ready when the baby wanted it.

Plucking the child from her crib, Lily was slightly more responsive than last night. Almost through instinct, the child sucked when the nipple rubbed her lips. But she drank little before she was asleep again.

All morning Sally tried waking her baby and feeding her. Gradually, the sedative effect dissipated, and Lily became more the child Sally recognized.

Maybe she hadn't used the correct dosage of Benadryl. On the other hand, it was good to be able to sleep.

Sally withdrew from the accounting class. She avoided Paige, silencing her calls, then blocking her number. Paige, the one person who'd believed in Sally. Sally could not face her friend now, ashamed to disappoint her friend and mentor.

Was it wrong to resent a baby? Well, she did. If not for this kid, she'd be well on her way to being a qualified book-keeper and maybe more. Didn't this kid realize that Sally was doing this for both of their sakes? She looked at the innocent child sleeping in her crib. The warmth didn't come. Am I becoming my mother?

Chapter Twenty-Four

There were men. Oh, not nearly as many as Izzy went through, and far fewer losers, but there were some. Sally prided herself on her pickiness, her taste in choosing partners, even if they didn't all work out.

Izzy was right about one thing - men had their uses. They made more money and were handy with sharing expenses. Some insisted on paying their way; others insisted on paying for everything. Sure, why not?

Lucas had potential.

He moved in two months ago. He was no Robert, the slow, steady type that had stayed with Izzy for several years now.

Rather than calming down a room, Lucas lit it up. He was a party all to himself.

When had life become such a drag? Over the last decade, it wore her down. That weight on her shoulders never slipped off.

That is, until she met Lucas. He didn't allow himself to

be mired in doldrums. He never wallowed; instead, he made things happen. Sometimes alcohol helped, sometimes other things elevated the mood. Life was simply more exciting with Lucas.

And he worked at a regular job, with a regular paycheck. He didn't make lawyer-style wages but did all right as a journeyman electrician. His job was tough, running a crew, training new guys, always responsible for their work.

Some days went well, others not so much. Those were the days when Sally needed to take care.

Lucas liked things quiet. Fair enough; so did Sally. The problem was Lily. She'd found her voice.

During her third year of life, Lily's vocabulary grew daily. She loved trying out her new words, the songs she learned at daycare, and asking that infernal 'why' question. Over and over and over until Sally wanted to scream.

But she didn't. She'd learned in her life that sucking it up was the best policy.

Lucas, not so much. As the youngest in his family, he'd not had to cater to others.

On the good days, he ignored Lily. That was fine; she ignored him, too. But this was not a good day.

A rookie had screwed things up at work, making Lucas work overtime to fix up his messes or the work wouldn't pass inspection. Lucas fired the kid, but he had to redo most of what the kid had attempted that week.

He got home late. Supper dried out long before he got there. The once bubbling hot lasagna now had a hard crust of dark brown cheese, with extra crispy pasta ends peeking out. There had been fresh parmesan cheese to go on top, but Lily spilled the container, dumping the expensive stuff all over the floor. As the child turned in her chair to survey the damage, her elbow tipped over her glass of milk, mixing the fluid in with now-soggy cheese. Parmesan could smell like baby puke at the best of times; when mixed with milk, the obnoxious odor permeated their small apartment.

That's what assaulted Lucas' senses when he turned his key in the lock and entered the room. That and Lily's wails.

Although the spill had been cleaned up hours ago, Lily remained out of sorts. She whined. She demanded to be picked up. She wanted a story. She wanted Paw Patrol. She wanted her mother.

But so did Lucas.

"Shut that kid up!" The look in Lucas' eyes brooked no argument.

Sally picked up her daughter and put her in the bedroom, shutting the door.

Lily had grown in the last few months and so had her manual dexterity. She was soon back in the living room, clamouring for her mom's attention. When Sally pushed her away, Lily wept - loud, moist wails with plenty of snot.

Sally shared the distaste that was clear on Lucas' face, but what could you do? Kids were not always controllable. Sally tried ignoring the toddler.

Lucas was having none of it. Neither was Lily.

"Get that kid out of here and shut her up." Lucas' eyes narrowed and his teeth clenched.

"How?" Sally was out of ideas.

"Either you shut her up or I will."

Now Sally sat up. Was he threatening her child? "Don't you *dare* touch my kid."

"What do you think I am? I might hate the brat but I'm not a child beater."

Sally relaxed somewhat, as much as she could with a howling toddler by her knees.

Lucas turned on the TV. "I'm warning you. Shut her up or you won't like what happens." He gave it three seconds, then his fist flashed out, catching Sally in the solar plexus.

She hunched over, struggling to catch a breath around the red-hot burning under her ribs. Her tiny squeaking noises stopped her daughter.

Lily took her thumb from her mouth and stared at her mother.

Lucas settled back, using the remote to shut off Paw Patrol and bring up the ball game.

The change on the screen started up Lily's protests again.

"I said to shut her up." This time, he didn't wait. His hand cuffed the side of Sally's head.

Ears ringing, the inside of her mouth bleeding, Sally froze, her eyes unfocused.

Lucas put his face near Lily's level. "Every time you utter a sound, your mom gets it. Hear me?"

Lily's watery eyes met his. Then her mouth opened, and a shriek came out at glass-shattering decibels.

Lucas grabbed the back of Sally's hair and smashed her face into the coffee table. "Is this what you want?" he asked Lily.

The evening wore on, Sally sometimes aware, sometimes not. Gradually, Lily got quieter. Every sound she made was met with quick reprisal from Lucas on her mother's body. Lily's three-year-old sense of empathy was in its developmental stages, but she got it. It took a number of relentless consequences, but Lily got it. By the time she put herself to bed, she made not a sound.

When Sally awoke the next morning, Lucas was gone. Alarmed, Sally checked that his stuff was still there. It was. He had left for work.

Her first attempt to leverage herself out of bed failed.

The next time she woke up, forty-five minutes had passed. She'd be late for work. Could she work like this?

Struggling, she made it to the bathroom, afraid to view the damage. Other than those first two blows, Lucas had left her face alone. Yeah, blood dried on her nose, and she had some bruises, but nothing makeup wouldn't hide. Or mostly hide.

The problem was the rest of her body. Lucas had gone after places that wouldn't show with her clothes on. Slowly, carefully, wincing, she removed her t-shirt and panties and inspected her body. It was mainly her torso that turned livid colors. Handprints showed in several places on her arms. Her throat ached and would need a turtleneck to hide the bruising. It hurt to breathe. She couldn't imagine ever eating again.

All this because her kid wouldn't stop crying.

Her kid! Where was Lily? Surely Lucas hadn't done something to her. He said he didn't beat children. But she didn't know he beat women, either.

In the living room, Lily sat scrunched up on the floor, the remote in her hand, eyes glued to the television screen. Paw Patrol.

"Lily?"

No answer.

Sally tried again, louder, forcing more air through her sore throat.

Lily turned her head, but neither smiled nor responded.

Easing onto the floor behind the child, Sally carefully

lifted Lily to her lap, gently cradling this warm bundle of humanity. Lily sank into her mother, thumb in her mouth.

"How's my big girl this morning?" Sally smoothed Lily's hair from her forehead.

No answer.

Turning the child to face her, Sally inspected her little girl. She seemed fine. "Do you hurt, baby?"

Nothing.

There were times in her life when Sally'd felt too traumatized to speak. Rocking her daughter to her, she allowed the child to deal with things in her own way. Silence was good. The opposite had brought last night's nightmare.

They were late now, late for daycare, and late for work. "Come on, my girl. We need to get ready."

Standing, Lily took her mother's hand and allowed herself to be led to the bathroom. But she uttered not a word.

A quiet, compliant child was easier to manage, anyway.

Applying the right amount of disguising makeup took time, time she didn't have today, but she dared not leave the house without this camouflage paint. The long-sleeved turtleneck sweater was a bit warm for this weather, but it couldn't be helped.

At the daycare, Lily waved goodbye to her mother, but didn't smile or say a word.

Walking from the daycare to work gave Sally some needed

thinking time. Mentally, she assessed what was in her bank account. Not enough.

The rent was due next week. If Sally paid it on her own, she'd be strapped, badly strapped, for the next two weeks. She needed Lucas to stay and pay the rent. She needed his money.

Chapter Twenty-Five

It took little to get rid of Lucas. After the rent was paid, of course. He was done with her, too, and needed scant persuasion to vacate the premises. He wanted a warm and willing bed partner, not the icicle he said she was.

There were other men, some nearly as bad as Lucas, some tolerable while they lasted.

Sally devised a test. After getting to know a man and after intimacy, she'd deliberately provoke him. Would he use his fists? Would he holler and swear? That she could live with, but never again would she allow herself to be beaten by a man. By anyone.

Assigned to the deli in the supermarket meant more interactions with the customers, more than just responding to where items were in the store. She got to know some of the regulars.

One man came in sporadically, then more and more often. He'd hang back until Sally was free to serve him. He asked her opinion on what was best that day, even though the selection never varied, and he'd sampled pretty much everything they carried.

One day, he waited, avoiding eye contact with any of the employees until there were no customers left. He scowled at a young girl working the counter and waited until Sally was free. After placing his order, he motioned her to the side. "Um, I was wondering what time you get off work. Would you like to have a coffee with me? There's a Starbucks around the corner." Blushing, he added, "You work here. Of course, you know what's near here."

He seemed like a nice guy. Good-looking, polite and with enough money to buy whatever he wanted from the pricey deli counter.

There was a deal-breaker, though. She had a kid. Too often she'd seen her mother drag home a man who was shocked to learn that Izzy lived with daughters. For Sally, it saved time if a guy knew upfront that she had Lily. Why invest time in a guy who'd run at first sight of a child?

"I'm off at six, but I have to pick up my daughter from daycare."

"We could go get her and take her with us. They have stuff that kids like at Starbucks." His brow wrinkled. "At least I think they do."

Sally nodded. "They do." But expensive things she'd never spent money on. Trusting her honed judgement, she decided. "Sure. We'd love to come with you."

His grin lit up the deli department. He reached his long arm over the counter. "I'm Carl. Pleased to meet you."

"I'm Sally." She pointed to her name tag. A line was

forming, so she had to get back to work. "I'll meet you at the front of the store a few minutes after six."

So began her romance with Carl. He was as good as he seemed. He was even nice to Lily, some evenings playing with her far more than Sally's patience ever allowed.

"Mom, could you babysit Lily tonight?" Rarely did Sally ask Izzy for help, but this was important, maybe the most crucial night of Sally's life.

"No. That's not my job. Your kid, you look after her. Besides, Robert and me have plans."

Robert cocked his head at Izzy. "What are you talking about, baby? We don't have any plans."

Izzy trailed her fingers up Robert's left arm and around the back of his neck. "I have plans for you." She planted a wet kiss on his neck.

Robert pulled away, frowning. To Sally, he said, "Of course we'll take care of the wee Lily. We'd love to have her."

"Thanks." Her smile took in Izzy as well as Robert, despite the malice flowing from Izzy. This was a big night, a big weekend. Lily would be fine for a few days, especially with Robert around.

A few hours later, Sally deposited a freshly bathed and pajama-clad Lily in her mother's living room. She gave the child a kiss and her favorite, scruffy teddy bear, then left before Izzy could ask any tricky questions like when she'd be back.

Soon, Carl arrived. Sally waited outside the apartment building's front door, her purse over one shoulder, a small suitcase at her feet.

Opening the trunk of his car, Carl deposited her suitcase with his own, then they were on their way. Vegas, baby.

Their first night was full of all the glitz and excitement Sally'd expected. But TV shows didn't portray what it was like to actually *be* there.

She spent the first twenty-four hours figuring things out. Where they'd go, how much alcohol was required and where to do the deed.

It took little, in fact, far less persuasion than Sally expected, and they were hitched. A genuine Vegas wedding after waiting in the lineup with several other couples.

Despite Carl's hangover, they drove home Sunday; he had work on Monday. Sally awoke Sunday morning with trepidation. Would Carl freak out when he realized they'd married?

Her fears were needless. At first, he blinked at the gaudy, paste ring Sally flashed his way. It took his booze-addled brain several seconds for reality to sink in. Then he pulled her into his arms. "My wife. I like the sound of that." He planted a big kiss on her lips, then they didn't leave the bed for some time.

It was late when they arrived back at Sally's apartment. Carl insisted on going with her to pick up Lily. "She's mine now, too."

It was Robert who opened the door, looking haggard and worn. Had Lily given them a hard time?

"No, your little one was sweetness. Can't say the same for her grandmother, though." He picked up a suitcase from inside the door, then made to move past Sally and Carl.

"Where are you going?"

"Out. I'm leaving. Your mom and I are through. I stood by while she's done a lot of things, things I didn't like. The worst is her treatment of you girls. She has no idea where Laura is. Bethany is gone half the time. She treats you like dirt after all you've done to keep her family together. Her refusal to babysit her own granddaughter was the last straw for me. Little Lily and me had a great time, but I can't be with a woman who treats her own kin so badly." He put his arm around Sally for a hug.

Carl stepped forward. "My name's Carl Hardy, sir. I'm Sally's husband."

Robert's smile was both sad and genuine. "You treat this little lady well. She's a gem."

"I plan to, sir."

"Sally, you've got my number. You ever need anything...."

Sally nodded, blinking back tears. She'd only known this man for four years, but he was the most she'd ever had for a father figure. The only good thing Izzy had done was introduce this man into their lives and now she'd screwed that up.

Chapter Twenty-Six

Carl had a house. Not much of a house and it was a rental, but still. Sally had never lived in a house, and a three-bedroom house at that.

It was a step up. Plus, since Carl had been paying the rent on his own anyway, he saw no reason to change that. If Sally bought their food and cooked, he'd manage all the rest.

Izzy was right; men certainly had their uses.

Sally's wardrobe expanded into the closet of the second bedroom. Never had she had so much disposable income, income to spend on herself.

YouTube taught her how to apply makeup, how to find her style, and she did. Not only did Carl's appreciative glances bolster her, but so did the looks from other men - strangers on the street, as well as customers at work.

She had more time, too. Carl insisted on taking Lily to the daycare center each morning, allowing Sally to sleep in, just a little. But a half-hour was a half-hour.

Evenings were better, too. Some nights, Carl spent more

time with Lily than he did with Sally. That was fine; she cherished "me" time.

Why had she ever thought that she needed to bust her butt at night school in order to have a life like this? All she needed was the right man.

They settled into a comfortable routine and the years went by. Occasionally, a "is this all there is?" thought flittered by, but was quickly subdued.

In bed one night, Carl's hand rubbed Sally's flat stomach. "Ever think about having another baby?" he asked while nuzzling her neck.

Sally froze. What? Another kid? Wasn't one enough? Lily was eight, and in school, and independent, liking her own space. She never said much, and that was fine with her mom, although Carl questioned it.

Sally thought back to those first few years when it was just her and Lily. The endless dreariness of being the sole carer for an infant, then a toddler. Even getting her hair brushed was a feat some days. And time to do her nails? Huh.

Carl waited for an answer.

How to play this? To be fair, Carl was good with Lily and took the child off Sally's hands much of the time. Did Carl have one of those stupid urges to see his own genes brought forth into the world? It might be a way to cement their relationship.

She turned on her side to face her husband. "Is that something you think about?"

"Yeah. A lot now. I never used to think about having a kid of my own, but since Lily, I realized I like kids. Really like them. I never knew her as a baby, but I miss having a toddler around." He raised Sally's chin, so their eyes met. "I think I'd like to have a baby with you."

"Then let's make one."

This pregnancy seemed easier, or maybe she knew what to expect this time. And she didn't have a ton of other duties at the same time. No attending medical appointments alone.

Once Carl saw the baby on ultrasound, he became all he-man. He insisted Sally quit work; after all, her main job now was building their child into the healthiest baby possible. That required rest.

He took on most of the household chores, other than cooking, not wanting Sally to exert herself. He dutifully followed the grocery lists Sally made up, never balking about the items or the cost. Finally, Sally could experiment with meals she found on the cooking shows. Some worked; some didn't, but she got to eat foods she'd only heard of before.

Despite Izzy's pronouncements about men being turned off by fat or pregnant women, that wasn't the case with Carl. She was his world, she and Lily.

And now Jordy. Jordy entered this world easier than Lily had done, but just as fast. Good. Sally didn't have time for a drawn-out labor.

Once home, Carl set her up on the couch with everything she could want around her. He and Lily brought the baby to her when he needed to be fed, but were quick to attend to his other needs. Carl took twelve weeks of paternity leave to help with the baby. Well, to look after the baby. After all, it was his idea to have a kid, so....

After the first month, they switched to bottle feedings. That way Sally could get some uninterrupted sleep at nights, with Carl and Lily taking turns warming the bottle and holding the baby.

It reduced their income with Carl on leave, but he never complained about her spending. They owed her, after doing all the work to bring this child into their lives.

It got harder. Carl returned to full-time work and Lily was away at school for almost seven hours a day. That left Sally alone with Jordy. The kid napped, or at least she made him remain in his bed for a spell each morning and afternoon. He couldn't open his bedroom door, and she needed her alone time.

Once Lily got home from school, Jordy's whole being beamed with delight at seeing his playmate. The first task Lily did was change her brother's diaper, then keep him entertained while Sally watched her soaps.

Sally got it now. She understood Izzy's insistence on her own fun money, her right to do what she wanted to after years of working and looking after others. It was only fair. The resentment Sally felt as a kid was unreasonable now that she looked back through an adult lens, a mother's lens. She'd put in her time. Some things are just owed.

But two was enough. She'd done her duty by Carl, allowing his genes to make their mark on the world. Her body had survived two pregnancies, holding up decently. Izzy warned her that a third made it much tougher to get back into shape. She might have snagged a man, but she still needed to keep him.

Carl believed her. The pill and IUDs were potentially harmful to a woman's body. Sally had endured them long enough. Tubal ligations were major surgery and came with risks. She explained these to Carl in as much graphic detail as possible:

- Infection.
- Bleeding from an incision or inside the abdomen.
- Side effects from anesthesia.
- Damage to other organs inside the abdomen. (Surgeries went wrong, you know.
- Ectopic pregnancy.

Carl was virile, she reminded him. She could still get pregnant, even after a tubal ligation, but the egg would become fertilized outside the uterus, resulting in a life-threatening situation for Sally.

The only solution was for Carl to have a vasectomy. Up to now, it was *her* body that had taken all the risks. Time for him to step up.

And he did.

Who knew that vasectomies weren't foolproof? You'd think snip, snip, then you're done. But oh, no, those sneaky sperm could linger, sometimes for months afterward. Up to three months, so the doctor said. He warned that if Carl had returned for his scheduled sperm check, they would have known when it was safe to have unprotected sex. But Carl hadn't wanted to jack off into a cup in any doctor's office. Now....

Baby Benjie came along when Jordy was midway through his second year of life. A life that was *busy*. Lily, at that age, was tame by comparison. Sally had to have Carl install a lock on the outside of Jordy's bedroom door to keep the kid in so that Sally could have some peace during the day.

Because Jordy didn't know his own strength and had the impulse control of his aunts Bethany and Laura, they could not leave the baby alone with him. The crib went into Lily's room. That worked, because Lily was close when the baby cried in the night.

Sally took out a gym membership. It was for Carl's sake, really; she had to get herself back into shape to look good for her man. Although the gym had babysitting services, it was a drag to cart a toddler plus a baby to the facility, even though Sally had a car of her own. Instead, it was simpler for everyone if Sally waited to leave until Lily got home from school.

Of course, that meant that supper would be very late.

It was time for Lily to step up. Sally'd been making the family dinners for ages by the time she was Lily's age. It was a good life skill for the kid to have.

Sally gave her a step up. She began by leaving the ingredients already prepared and ready to be assembled. Gradually, Lily learned how to peel vegetables and to follow a recipe. Things didn't always work out, and Sally had to rag on her far more often than should be necessary, but over time, Lily got the hang of it. Mostly.

Chapter Twenty-Seven

It all went well until it didn't.

It wasn't really anyone's fault. Truly, it wasn't Carl's fault, but how not to blame him? It wasn't his fault that his company went into receivership. How could he not have seen this coming? Sure, lots of companies struggled during these economic times, but wasn't that a man's job to be on top of such things? To jump ship before everything collapsed? To ensure a steady income for his family?

It was obvious that Carl felt badly. His constant apologizing got on her nerves. His hangdog expression was worse each day he came home, reporting that no, he'd not found another job.

As prospects worsened, Carl hung out at the day job depot, where employers would pick up men to do odd jobs for the day. The pay was lousy and irregular. The amount of spending money in their account vanished faster than deals on Black Friday. Soon it cut into their lifestyle. Sally's lifestyle.

As if all this wasn't bad enough, Carl came asking for a favor. Begging, actually.

"I'm sorry, but it's my brother." Carl's bloodshot eyes were more dismal than normal. "He needs a place to stay. His girlfriend kicked him out, and he's coming after work today."

What? Where did he think they'd put the guy?

"I thought we'd move Lily into the boys' room. She spends a lot of her time in there with them, anyway. Then Archie can have her room."

Whatever. Who cared which room Lily slept in? But another mouth to feed? It had been years since she'd seen Archie, but he was a big guy. That meant he'd eat a lot. "Will he pay his way?"

Carl nodded. "He knows I'm out of a job and things are tough for us. He says that he'll pay the rent."

"The full rent?"

"Yep."

Archie's temporary move became semi permanent. He took up a lot of space, just his presence, let alone his things. Archie owned any room he was in.

He may have lost a girlfriend, but his self-confidence never faltered.

He worked shift. That meant he was often home in the day while Carl was out wearing off the soles of his shoes, hunting that elusive job. So Archie and Sally spent more and more time together and became closer.

Initially, they skirted around one another, while Carl tried to bring the two closer. The most important people in his life should be friends, he said. He got his wish. Through proximity and time, Sally's and Archie's comfort level with each other increased. Shared interests and shared needs.

Archie brought the excitement into Sally's life, excitement that she'd sorely missed. After work, Archie enjoyed going to the pub. It was only right that he let Sally tag along; she needed a break, too. Soon it was a regular thing for them, their daily or nightly outings for a drink or two, or three.

Their outings ended well, with Sally bubbly and amorous.

Archie wanted more. He complained he paid for everything around here, but got none of the benefits. It was imperative for their family's well-being to keep Archie happy and with them.

Things progressed from the odd stolen smooch or feel, to cuddles on the couch, to Sally spending most nights in Archie's bed. All for the sake of the family.

All went well until Lily messed it up. Puberty struck, and with it Lily developed early, just like her mom had done. At first, there were some snide comments. Sally laughed but kept her eye on things. Carl, clueless, still thought of Lily as his little girl.

But Sally noticed the changes in Archie. He watched the girl more and more, his eyes following her as she bent over to pick up her littlest brother.

Although he mostly ignored the little boys, he now paid attention to Lily, holding out his arm for her to come sit with him on the couch to watch television. Initially, Lily complied, but then she started avoiding eye contact with her step-uncle, leaving the room when he entered, making a wide arc when she had to pass by him.

Sally knew the signs. She'd been there, as had Laura. It was only a matter of time before Lily snagged Archie's attention away from Sally. If he fancied Lily and left with her, where would that leave the rest of them? Besides, what Archie planned to do with Lily was not something any preteen needed to suffer.

It was a mother's duty to protect her children. She had three of them. There was only one man around to support them, and she couldn't risk losing that.

There was only one thing she could do.

Chapter Twenty-Eight

Plans were funny things. They rarely turned out the way they were supposed to.

Plans were all she had at one time, plans to clean the apartment, plans to make a meal out of nothing, plans to stretch an impossibly small budget, plans to get through the day.

Then they grew more grandiose. Go to college, get a diploma in accounting, create a career for herself and never have to worry about money again.

Well, life had a way of interfering with plans.

This time, though, maybe it was all for the best.

Archie kept their family afloat. Carl may not be at his happiest, but who was? He didn't need to send her those hurt puppy dog looks. She was doing the best she could for all of them.

The hitch, though, was Lily. She attracted more and more of Archie's attention. If Lily replaced Sally in Archie's affections, what would that mean for their family? Would he withdraw his money? Plus, as a good mother, of course Sally did not want Lily, innocent Lily to go through what she and Laura had at the hands of their mother's boyfriends.

Innocent Lily. Sally watched covertly. Was Lily innocent or was she leading Archie on? There was too much at stake. Lily would have to go.

The plan might not be perfect, but it was all she had.

You couldn't just ditch a child, everyone knew that. And Sally didn't want harm to befall her daughter. After weeks of thinking, Sally hit upon the perfect plan. She needed a safe place to take Lily. School was out because they knew where she lived and would bring her right back home. Sally considered taking the girl to a cop shop and letting her off there, but Sally'd never felt comfortable around officers of the law.

The closest place she could find was the courthouse. Was there anyplace safer for a young girl? The place reeked of law people – judges, lawyers, guards and who knows who else – all people in positions to help. Yeah, dumping her there was a stoke of genius. They'd look after her. Bonus was Lily's silence. Although she rarely spoke these days, just the added inducement of the ill that would befall her mother if Lily opened her mouth or disclosed her identity was enough to keep the kid silent.

Lily was gone, safe from Archie's clutches. Carl remained with her and the boys, and Archie, of course, and continued to pay their way.

Then Carl had to mess things up, Carl and Lily's nosy teacher. She told Carl and told him that Lily was fine, but oh no. He and that stupid teacher woman had to go to the police, reporting Lily missing. It took time, but somehow it got out that Sally was Lily's mother and that the child found wandering the courthouse halls was Lily.

Nothing much happened beyond some dirty looks from the cops, but she was used to that. Who cared what they thought?

Lily landed on her feet. She stayed in a place larger than most homes Sally observed on TV. She was with professionals, wealthy ones at that, ones who never had to worry about where their next paycheck was coming from. Anna and that Murph guy had it easy, and now Lily got to share in their good life. So what if that high-and-mighty social worker, Anna, changed Lily's name? Who cared? Bonnie, Lily, what's the difference?

The judge ordered visits. Sally could do that. Plus, she brought along the boys and Lily/Bonnie looked after them. Bonus!

Once, just once at a visit in the park, Sally had to do a quick errand in the car. Lily was with the boys; they were fine, having the time of their lives playing on the swings. But those stupid foster parents, Anna and Murph, had to show up early. They had the nerve to call the police, saying Sally abandoned her kids. The nerve! Well, they got through that one, and visits were now at Anna and Murph's house, under their nosy eyes.

Like today. But just how much time could you spend with kids? Lily was quiet, but those boys. Jordy rarely shut up. Baby Benjie couldn't really talk but made up for it with his noises and shrieks. Good thing Lily tolerated them. And the dogs. There were two of them, dirty things - one a German Shepherd, the other some Corgi thing that looked like it would have been a regular dog if someone hadn't cut its legs off short.

Despite all that room in the house, plus an acreage to spread out in, Anna was picky. No smoking in the house. She relegated Sally to a spot outside on the patio, with an ashtray, smoking under supervision, while Anna watched from the window. Sure, she said she was watching the kids play, but like, who'd believe that?

Benjie and the little dog came running by. Benjie put his dirty hands on her clothes; he'd been playing in the dirt and now her ecru skirt had brown streaks. Filthy child. She stood, brushing at the fabric with the backs of her hands. Ruined. Then that stupid dog, the little one with half-legs, jumped up on her, its disgusting paws furthering the ruination of her skirt. Shoving him off, the beast flopped onto his side, spilling into the ashtray. Butts went between the flagstones, on top of them, and into the grass.

Let Anna clean this up. She was out of there.

She strolled down the driveway to the path that wound around the meadow. There were other homes on this street, although not many, since each owned five-acre lots. How could they stand to live in a place like this? It was almost rural. Only a few houses on the whole road, dirt and grassy pasture, and no sidewalks. If you wanted to go anywhere, you had to walk on the street. And what was there to do? Just how many blades of grass could you look at? One enormous tree dominated the grassy area, looking out of place. The kids congregated there for some reason. Yeah, it provided shade, but to get there, you had to walk through long grass. Who knew what lurked there?

Out of place in this semi-isolated area was a car, a grey SUV parked facing Anna and Murph's house, but half a block away.

Approaching that SUV, she was curious. Why was it parked here in the middle of the boonies? It was about halfway between Murph's property and the next acreage. The driver held the map against his steering wheel but wasn't looking at it. Instead, he was watching the three children playing in the meadow. Staring at them, actually. Every few moments, his attention would be drawn to the house, then back to the kids. Weird.

Sally slowed as she neared the vehicle. That was one fine looking specimen of manhood, and all she could see were his shoulders and head. She put a little more hip movement into her stride. Yes, now he noticed her, although he seemed to divide his attention between the playing kids and her. Well, she could fix that.

She strolled around the front of the car to the driver's side window. Leaning down, she peered in at him. "Hey, there."

The window rolled half-way down. The man eyed the bosom that was in front of his face.

"Are you looking for someone?" Sally wiggled just a little as she said that. Yes, she had his attention now. It was firmly fixed on a part of her anatomy, of which she was particularly proud.

"I'm always on the lookout for that special someone," replied Alejandro. He gave her a knowing smile. "Are you special?"

"So they tell me."

"What are you doing way out here?"

"I'm doing a visitation thing with my kid." She pointed out the window. "See that girl out there? That's my Lily. Well, she goes by the name Bonnie now." She looked coyly at Alejandro. "Do you think I'm old enough to have a daughter that age?"

Alejandro laughed. He hit the automatic unlock button. "Are you finding it hot in the sun? Why not sit in here and enjoy the air conditioning?"

"Don't mind if I do." Sally got in, making sure that her skirt rose to just the right height on her legs. Then she put one knee over the other.

Alejandro's look said that he appreciated the sight. His attention was pulled again toward the kids as an especially loud giggle reached them.

Sally noticed that his eyes mostly followed Bonnie. "She's beautiful, isn't she? Takes after her mother."

Alejandro's hand brushed over Sally's thighs as he reached into the glove box, pulling out a pair of binoculars. He raised them to his eyes and adjusted the focus. "Yes, she's a good-looking girl. In some circles she'd be highly sought after."

Sally eyed him. Alejandro was watching Bonnie in an assessing way, but not with the same leers that Archie had given her. No, Sally did not think that Bonnie was her rival with Alejandro. But he was definitely interested in her. Why?

A large truck drove by, slowing as it approached, the driver taking in every detail of Alejandro's SUV. The truck kept going, turning into Anna and Murph's driveway. The man opened his door, talking and holding a phone to his ear. His eyes didn't leave the silver RAV4. A woman got out of the passenger side and opened the back door, leaning in. She soon emerged with a small boy. As soon as he climbed out, he raced to meet the other children playing in the field. While the woman went into the house, the man started toward Alejandro's car.

"Babe, I think it's time for me to get out of here. You coming?" He started the car.

"Sure." Sally reached for her seatbelt and snapped it into place. "This place is too tame for me."

Alejandro gave her knee a squeeze, then pulled away from the curb, heading away from the man. Alejandro wasn't sure, but he thought the man had just snapped a picture of the back of his car.

Alejandro grinned at Sally. Maybe this day was not a lost cause. This woman looked a little old, a little saggy and a little sad. But she still had potential and the right attitude. "Are you up for a little fun?"

"Sure. Always." Sally's reply held no hesitation.

They sat on the same side of the plush upholstered bench in the hotel's lounge. This time of day, there were few customers and the corner booth felt private.

Alejandro was getting a good feeling about this woman. While Anna had not fallen in with his plans as easily as he had hoped, he might have just found a replacement. He wasn't that picky; he simply needed someone to keep the girls in line.

This first stage of the dance, though, required some effort on his part. He could charm when he tried, of that he was confident. So far, it seemed to be working. Now to see what would lure her in.

Reaching into his back pocket, he pretended his phone had vibrated, and he checked the message. "Nothing," he said. "Nothing as important as you." He smiled.

Sally simpered, or at least Alejandro was pretty sure that

was the word to describe her reaction to his compliment. Yes, she would be easy to manipulate.

Sliding his finger up on his iPhone, he knew what might reel her in. "Want to see some pictures of my place?"

"Oh course." Sally leaned closer, her chest resting on his upper arm.

"I have a little place in the hills." He knew his estate was impressive by almost anyone's standards. This woman hanging on his arm didn't look like she had much acquaintance with wealth or class. Turning his phone to landscape view to better see the pictures, he showed her the perfectly landscaped grounds with the flower beds, fountains, cabana and pool, flagstone patio and sheltered gazebo.

Her eyes got larger with each one. Alejandro didn't tell her how cheap the labor was to maintain the place in this pristine condition. The photos didn't show the high concrete block walls, nor the razor wire along the top.

"Where *is* this place?" Sally asked.

"In Mexico, not too far over the border. It's in the mountains, and the climate is perfect." He opened another album on his phone. He'd done this many, many times. It always worked; women fell for the place and came willingly. "Want to see the inside?"

"Ooo, yes, of course."

If Sally had thought the grounds were something, she was in awe of the high ceilings, the tiled floors, and the sheer size of the place. "How many bedrooms?"

"Ten, although only three of them are suites."

"Who cleans the place?"

"I have an excellent staff. The head maid and the cook run the place, really. They keep the rest of the staff in line."

"Staff? How many are there?"

Alejandro shrugged. "I'm not sure. I've never counted.

Juana and Josefina run things for me. They do the hiring. I have a bookkeeper who keeps track of payroll." Among other stuff, he thought to himself.

"What I wouldn't give to see a place like that." A bookkeeper. What if something happened to that bookkeeper and a replacement stepped in?

"Maybe you will someday, maybe you will." He finished the last of his whiskey and soda. The noise level in the lounge rose as the after-work crowd came in. "Would you like to go upstairs? I have a nice suite."

Chapter Twenty-Nine

Sometimes, when you just know something's right, you have to act on it.

This Alejandro guy, he had his act together. He had the money, the lifestyle, the whole thing going on. Enough of this eking out a living. Working with Alejandro would give her everything she'd dreamed of. She could keep books. She could look after the girls who worked for him; she'd certainly done enough of that in her life.

There were a few more details Alejandro needed to get straight. Time to be blunt. "What about your kids?"

Yes, that thought had crossed Sally's mind. She kept trying to shove it away. This was her time. She'd spent enough years devoting herself to kids. Carl was the one who wanted children. Let him look after them.

"How old is your daughter?" Alejandro made sure his voice sounded casual.

"Twelve." While the girl was useful in looking after the

little boys and around the house, having a teen in her home, or an almost teen, was uncool. People would think *she* was old enough to have a kid of that age. When Lily/Bonnie was young, people made such a fuss over how pretty she was. But now, the kid was starting to rival Sally herself. Especially with Archie. Ah, but she'd not have to worry about that anymore if she went with Alejandro. Archie could do what he wanted.

"Twelve," said Alejandro. "That's a little young for baby-making, no?"

"Yeah, a bit, although some girls have kids when they're in their early teens." Sally eyed the man beside her. "Why?"

"Just wondering. If she was a little older, maybe she might have joined our stable. You know, had a nice life with us and produced some babies. Girls have them so easily when they're young and nubile."

Sally was catching on to something. "These adoptions. Do they pay a lot?"

Looking directly at her, Alejandro confirmed it. "Yes. A lot."

"Is it only babies they pay for?"

"In the past, yes, but we are thinking of branching out. There are other, ah, markets and families looking for older children." He left it hanging.

"What kind of people?"

"Wealthy people, very wealthy people. Ones who hand over cash and are well able to provide for a child."

Sally thought of the way she'd grown up. The life her children were experiencing was not much different. What if, in exchange for some nice money, she could guarantee that each of her kids could grow up in luxury? "What kind of money?"

"This is a new venture for us, so I am not as certain

about the price as I am for newborns. If I had to guess, I'd say somewhere in the nature of fifty thousand for a healthy child."

A swift thought flittered through Sally's brain - too bad she hadn't had more kids. "So I'd get fifty grand and my kid would get a wonderful home and a rich life." Bonus, her kids would luxuriate in similar styles. No more growing up in poverty for them. Didn't a mother owe it to her children to give them that opportunity?

"*We'd* get fifty grand. There are expenses I'd need to take out of that sum and a finder's fee."

"Yes, of course."

"And once the money changes hands, we cannot guarantee what happens. But then, you had no guarantee when you had a baby just what kind of life he would have. All I can guarantee is that it would be a wealthy home."

"Money matters."

"Yes, it does."

"My Lily. I have a worry about her. She is, ah, blossoming, becoming a woman. She's a beautiful girl. Her stepfather's brother, Archie, stays with us. He's taken an interest in her and not an uncle kind of interest, if you know what I mean. That's why I had to get her out of the house, for her own protection. That's why she's staying with Anna right now. If I left and Bonnie went back home, I would worry about her safety."

"A mother would worry about her child. By all means, bring her with you, if that would make you feel better. We'll find a place for her."

Plans. They took time, but over the next months, they took shape. Yeah, they involved effort, but they also involved air travel, a first for Sally. They involved a mansion, and soon, when her children were relocated to their new homes, more wealth than she'd every imagined.

When in her life had her plans worked out, no matter how hard she tried? When all looked rosy, things went to hell.

It was that damned Anna. She screwed up everything. Why'd she have to stick her nose in? They weren't even *her* kids; they were Sally's and she could do with them what she wanted.

Anna cost her big, made her lose a lot of money and the best job imaginable.

At least she had the money from the sale of the boys, even if Anna stole Bonnie right from under their noses.

Alejandro mirrored plus amplified Sally's hate for Anna. Thanks to Anna, his principal business shut down, and he was in hiding. Mind you, he hid in style, thankfully, since Sally hid with him.

Over time, Alejandro changed. Rather than treating Sally as his woman, his partner, he relegated her to an employee. Overlooking his slights, there would be a way back into his number one spot. He'd see he couldn't do without her.

Men were fickle creatures. For Alejandro, revenge took over. All he could think about, talk about, was Anna and what he'd do to her. Oh, he was smart and patient. Revenge best served cold and all that. He knew Anna from way back, knew that the best way to hurt her was through those she loved, knocking away at her heart a little at a time, until the organ collapsed under its burden.

To serve his kind of justice took planning. She could live with that and even help. But why did he have to treat her like a servant? She'd go along with it, but only so far. After all, she had money of her own now and would only take so much from any man.

But it had gone wrong, so wrong. That snake, Alejandro fled with his so-called daughter, leaving Sally to take the fall. She'd not even known what the plans were, so how could they blame her? The cops didn't get it. *She* was a victim here. A sentence of five years was far too harsh. The California Institute for Women was so not what she'd envisioned as her new home.

Part III

Chapter Thirty

"I hate feeling like this." Anna, usually the most charitable of women, struggled with the unkind thoughts she had toward Sally. "I know she's Bonnie's mother and has rights, but what about the rights of the child? Bonnie deserves to be happy, to be settled."

"You're right." Murph put his arms around Anna and rested his chin on her head. "This is what the courts have ruled though, and Sally gets to have contact with her daughter."

Anna pulled back a bit in his arms so that she could see Murph's face. "But she'll hurt Bonnie, I know she will."

Murph nodded. "Can't see how it will end up any other way; it always has in the past, at least as long as we've known the two of them." He drew Anna closer. "Guess that's where we come in. We'll be here to pick up the pieces, give her the security she needs."

"Judge Bursey should know better than this."

"It's out of his hands."

"I know all the theory," said Anna. "About how it's

better for a child to learn what their parent is really like, even if they get hurt in the process. Better for them to have access and suffer disappointment, than to believe 'the system' kept them apart. Better than believing some fantasy about the parent. But it's different when that kid is Bonnie."

"So true. But we've seen just what a strong kid she is. She'll survive, and she has us."

"I can't believe that Sally is Bonnie's mother. There isn't a kinder, more giving child than Bonnie. How could she come from such a woman?"

"It is hard to imagine. Bonnie is nothing like her mother."

"Do you think Sally will ever change?"

"Who knows? We don't know what she was like at Bonnie's age."

"Do life's events shape us, or do they bring out who we were all along?"

Bonnie sat directly in front of the laptop screen. She and Anna had checked that all the technology was ready to go half an hour ago, even practiced with Murph from his office via Zoom. The prison didn't use Zoom, as they deemed it not secure enough, but had their own Webex system. The prison social worker would be on hand if Sally had tech difficulties, to check Bonnie's and Anna's identification, and to monitor what they said. Perhaps one day unsupervised virtual visits would be allowed, but not yet. Lily was a minor, and Sally had to prove herself first.

Then Sally's upper body filled the screen. "Lily, my baby girl! You look so grown up! Oh, I've missed you so much. It's *so* good to see you."

Well, thought Anna, it had been eight months since

Sally had last been in the same city as Lily, and at that time, she'd made no effort to contact her only daughter. They'd last seen each other in Mexico, on Alejandro's compound, where Sally attempted to sell her children. Now, Lily, (who preferred to be called Bonnie), and Jordy lived with Anna and Murph as foster children.

Lily/Bonnie smiled shyly at her mother.

"So, Lily, tell me all about your day. How's school?" Sally waited, her smile slipping a bit as her questions met with silence.

Anna inched her chair closer, her hands on Bonnie's shoulder. She placed her face within the camera's view finder, giving a warning glance at Sally.

Sally's laugh was unpleasant. "Still stubborn, are you girl? Still refusing to answer your mother?"

The prison social worker stepped in. "Sally, we talked about this. You'll need to take the lead in the conversation. If you make your daughter too anxious, or too uncomfortable, these visits may have to stop."

Sally glared at Anna. "I suppose *you* have a say in that?"

"I can offer my opinion. Bonnie's well-being is my priority."

Sally shook this off, and a new smile appeared on her face. She tried again. "I was thinking about you last night, about the day you were born. You were the sweetest little thing."

Bonnie smiled. The resemblance between her and her mother clearer.

"I wish I had some pictures of you from back then, but I have nothing like that with me in this place. They don't let me have much of anything here." She took a sip from the styrofoam cup of tepid coffee on the table in front of her. "Why don't you send me some photos?"

Bonnie's kind eyes flicked to Anna, then back to her mom. Her mouth opened, but nothing came out. Helplessly, she looked at Anna.

Anna bit back the retort that welled up in her gut. Sally had abandoned Bonnie at the courthouse when the child was ten years old, leaving her to wander alone, until Anna noticed her. No clothing, no food, no identification, and certainly no family pictures. Putting on her big girl panties, Anna determined to be the adult, especially in front of Bonnie. "She doesn't have any pictures from her life with you."

"Oh, well, things get lost over time. We moved so many times, you know. Moving is such a pain."

Sally moved on to the crappy coffee they served in this joint, barely warm and weak. Not even real cream. "Maybe you could bring me a Starbucks, one day."

Lily/Bonnie nodded eagerly.

"That would be good. My only bright spot in this hell hole. You have no idea the slop they try to feed me here. No concern for what all those carbs will do to a woman's figure. Maybe it's a good thing I can barely choke it down. A woman could starve in a place like this."

Bonnie looked to Anna's kitchen where the aromas of a simmering beef soup wafting over.

The prison social worker intervened. "Our fifteen minutes is up."

Is that all it had been, thought Anna? An excruciating quarter hour of never knowing what Sally might say, or how it might affect Bonnie.

"I don't like these phone calls from Sally." Anna and Murph

lay in bed after the kids were asleep. "She asked Bonnie for money."

"There's no way to censor what that woman is saying to Bonnie." Murph rubbed the bridge of his nose. "Good thing she only gets to make one fifteen-minute call every two weeks."

"And her calls never last the fifteen minutes. It's hard to carry on a one-sided conversation with someone who has selective mutism, and seeing only their face to know how they're reacting." A part of Anna felt for Sally, the social worker therapist part. But right now, Anna was in mama-bear mode, wanting to protect her foster daughter.

"We know that woman is a master manipulator. She's not shown evidence of having Bonnie's best interests at heart, ever."

"So much of how we process things is through language. Bonnie doesn't have that advantage."

"That's why her therapist used art and play in their sessions."

"Still, there's a difference in Bonnie when she interacts with her mother. She withdraws."

"Maybe that's her way of working through things."

"Likely, but she also withdraws from Jordy." Overjoyed to be reunited with her little brother, the one she'd been like a mother to, Bonnie'd come alive when Jordy joined their household. From being childless and newly a couple, Anna and Murph were now foster parents to the brother and sister.

"I wish I was confident that Sally won't mess with Bonnie's mind."

Chapter Thirty-One

Other inmates received regular visits from family. They had family who *wanted* to see them. Izzy avoided unpleasantness and prison visits hit the top of that list. Bethany had her own life and Laura, well, no one knew where Laura was.

Carl, sweet Carl, turned out to not be so sweet. He came once to spew all over Sally, nasty stuff about their sons. What did Carl know about being poor? Could he not see that she'd given their boys the best shot at living a glorious life?

Visits broke the monotony. It was tough living through other people's visits, pretending indifference, when any bits of news from the outside world filled a vacuum.

Today, though, Lily was coming.

Julie plunked herself down beside Sally, uninvited, as usual. Somehow, Julie had attached herself to Sally, giving an imitation of a friend. "Are you excited about your girl coming today?"

Sally shrugged. Best to not give anything away in here. You never knew what they could use against you.

"Are you worried that she might be scared? The first time I visited my Bobby when he was locked up, I nearly peed my pants going through all the check-ins."

"Lily's tough. She'll do what she has to do."

Two o'clock arrived. Best not to look too eager. Didn't want to get the kid thinking she had power over her mother.

And there she was, the lone child sitting at a table, staring at her clenched hands. Yeah, well, this was a scary place. In the middle of the table sat a cardboard cup with the Starbucks logo on it.

"Lily."

The child's face lit up as her mother slid into the chair across from her.

"How are you?"

The kid's smile slipped a bit.

"Still not talking?" Hidden under the table, Sally's thumb rubbed back and forth against the side of her finger.

Still nothing, but Lily returned to studying her fists.

"Are you going to ask me how I am?" Without waiting for the response she knew wouldn't be coming, Sally continued. "I'm well, thanks for asking. Do you see the duds they make me wear in here?" She plucked at the short sleeves of her orange scrubs. "Not really my color, is it?" Well, this was exasperating. How could she have forgotten how annoying it was to try to have a conversation with this kid? She removed the lid from the coffee container and sipped. "Yuk. It's cold."

Lily/Bonnie's shoe beat a tattoo against the chair leg.

Sally tried again. "Did you bring the money?"

Lily nodded rapidly, and far longer than the answer required.

"Well, where is it?"

Lily half-turned in her chair, her chin pointed to the door she'd come in.

"Ah, the guards have it?"

Again, a nod, a more normal one this time.

"Wonder if I'll ever see it?"

Lily's brow wrinkled.

"They pinch stuff, you know. Bunch of thieves in this place."

Moisture pooled in the bottom of Lily's eyes. A look she'd perfected as a toddler, one that used to work on her mother before she wised up.

"How much did you bring?"

Lily swallowed and shot a quick look at her mother before studying her hands some more. "All."

"Ah, you can speak when you want to." All. Who knew how much that was from a kid? All was fine. Lily lived with rich people. Anna and Murph would refill her piggybank in no time.

"Do you want to ask me how I spend my days in here?"

Back to nodding, Lily's head bobbed.

"Still won't talk, eh? Well, this is pointless." Sally stood up. "Come back when you're willing to have a conversation like a normal person." Catching a guard's eye, she motioned to the door. This visit was over.

Watching her daughter's retreating back and drooping shoulders, Sally hunched in on herself. For just a minute, she forgot the bravado front she put up for all to see.

A guard tugged on her arm. "Your visit's over. Back to the dorm now."

Lying on her bed, Sally placed her arm over her eyes. Footsteps approached. Julie. It had to be. No one else would dare approach Sally when she gave out her 'leave me alone' vibes.

"Go away."

"But…,"

"GO AWAY!" Pulling her arm away, the look in her eyes conveyed a menace her words only hinted at.

Alone again, her mind took over. Oh, to be back in her apartment alone. Privacy. Her things. A life to do over.

She'd tried, really, she had. She knew what she wanted out of life and went after it. She deserved more, so much more than had been handed to her.

She thought back to those earlier times.

For a while, she'd thought she found the answer in Carl. He idolized her. He provided for her, at least until he didn't. Maybe it wasn't his fault that his company folded. Maybe he'd have gotten another job soon, a better job, but what was she supposed to do in the meantime?

Carl's brother, Archie, moving in was a godsend. Archie had a job, a good job, and he wasn't afraid to spend money. He kept their family afloat and asked little in return other than a place to sleep and a warm bedmate.

Yeah, Carl hadn't liked that part, but what was Sally to do? Sleeping with Archie meant that he'd fund her family. Besides, there was something exciting about that man, something that kept her on edge. Boring, he was not.

For a while it had worked. Then she noticed the way Archie looked at Bonnie. At first, it was out the side of his eyes when he thought no one was looking. Then his glances got bolder, as did his hands.

Growing up with her mother's revolving door of boyfriends, both Sally and Laura quickly learned to judge a man's intent and to stay clear of his touches. Mostly. Sally had been better at that than Laura and when Sally moved out, Laura endured these unwanted attentions.

Laura. No one knew where she was, or at least that's what Izzy said - on the streets somewhere, the ungrateful girl.

But Laura was no longer Sally's problem. Lily was. Lily hadn't had the experiences of Sally and Laura. She shied away from Archie, but probably didn't know what was in store for her.

A good mother protects her children. Right? They'd needed Archie and his money. There were the little boys, herself, and Carl, to think of. But Lily, she couldn't let Archie get his hands on her.

So, she did the best thing possible. She set Lily free.

What safer place in the world than a courthouse? There were lawyers and judges and guards all over the place. Her girl would be safe there. Someone would take care of her, make sure she was safe and away from Archie's clutches.

Good thing Lily hardly ever spoke. There was little danger that she'd give her own name, let alone Sally's. Lily would never get her mother in trouble, or so she'd believed. It would have worked, too, if not for Carl and that stupid teacher.

After dropping Lily off at the courthouse, Sally had driven three blocks, turned a corner, and pulled over. Resting her face in her hands, her forehead on the steering wheel, she sobbed. Sobbed for the childhood she herself had lost, sobbed for ever present burden of not enough money, sobbed for all the men who had let her down, sobbed for the loss of her first-born child.

When the storm within had passed, Sally mopped her face. Angling the rear-view mirror so she could see what she was doing, Sally repaired her makeup, hopefully removing all traces of emotion, then went home to Archie.

Chapter Thirty-Two

Peace. Solitude. Sally yanked her mind back. Why go there when those things were impossible in this place? "Live in the moment," the group therapist said. Yeah, right. She got to leave this place every day after work. *She* got paid to be here.

Still, it was decent advice. It was pointless to dwell on what ifs and what might have been. Try as she might, Sally's brain kept flitting back to previous times, times when she was freer.

Abhorring the constant motion, the constant noise, the never-ending pressure of people around her in this prison, Sally fled to the illusion of privacy her cot gave her. An arm across her face signalled to all to keep away. Sometimes it worked.

Still, Sally's brain insisted on returning to previous times. She thought about the apartment she had all to herself when Lily was born. Well, not all to herself because the kid was with her, but at that time, the baby stayed mostly in her crib. When Lily slept, Sally could imagine that she had the entire space to herself.

Clenching her fists, she dragged her mind from those memories, memories so different from her current situation. The dormitory in the California Institution for Women was crowded, beyond crowded, for someone who craved her own space.

Women. Other than her mother and sisters, Sally had little experience with women, apart from on a superficial basis. Now, she rubbed shoulders, literally, with dozens of them all day long.

At first it was tough. Unwritten social rules abounded. Inmates who'd been there awhile seemed to know how to enforce those rules. Newbies often picked them up quickly and soon fit in. To Sally, mixing with women was new, but she was strong on survival and learned.

Julie, for some unknown reason, attached herself to Sally, almost from the beginning. Julie – young, naïve, wouldn't take a hint. Clingy, too. Tolerating Julie felt like being with her younger sisters. But Julie's advice helped, even when Sally didn't want nearly so much of it.

Plunking herself down on the bench opposite Sally, Julie offered half of her candy bar. "There's someone I think you should meet."

Julie was always trying to expand Sally's circle of friends.

"Her name's Mimi. I think the two of you have a lot in common."

Sally quirked a brow.

"Like you, she's been screwed over by a man."

Sally laughed. "Tell me who in here hasn't been?"

"See, here's what I know about Mimi. She used to be married."

"Didn't we all?"

"Yeah, but her husband was a real dirt bag."

Sally rolled her eyes. As she got up, Julie rushed on.

"Her husband's an accountant."

Interesting.

"Mimi worked with him. They embezzled money from the investment firm they worked for. Her husband took off and left Mimi holding the bag. That's why she's in here."

Like Alejandro had done to Sally.

"Now, she's out for revenge."

Julie was right - having friends had advantages. Solo inmates didn't fare so well in this place. While Julie was more of a hanger-oner, Mimi appealed to Sally.

The woman had brains. She had plans and wouldn't be in her current situation for the rest of her life. She'd do it without needing a man to do it for her. Over the next year, Mimi and Sally became as close as Sally had ever been with anyone.

"Jeff thought he was the brains of our operation," confessed Mimi. "I let him believe that. What did it matter? Besides, he was cocky; that left me more time to make my own plans. I just didn't think he'd screw me over quite this bad, or quite so soon."

"What did he do?"

"His girlfriend pressed him to take the money and leave now."

"His girlfriend?"

"Yeah. News to me, too. Guess I had my head so firmly in the books that I didn't see what was in front of my nose."

She pursed her lips in disgust at herself. "She was a CPA with another firm. She helped Jeff lay a series of clues pointing back to me as the one doing the embezzling."

"Weren't you?"

"Hell, yeah, but not in the stupid way she laid out. I'd never be that sloppy."

"That's how you got caught?"

"She called it in, then skipped town with Jeff."

"*They* didn't get caught?"

Mimi shook her head. "But here's the thing. Jeff thought he took all the money."

"He didn't?"

"He only knew about a fraction of it. He thought he had it all, thought *I* was the sucker."

"You still have it?"

"It's safe until I get out of here and growing all the time."

"So, you'll just go get it when you're out of here?"

"It's not quite that simple. I need to set some things up. I'll need help."

Sally's head tilted, and she narrowed her eyes. "Help?"

"Yeah, I'd like a couple of people with me. I'll make it worth their while. Interested?"

"Does the Pope wear funny hats?"

"You're good with numbers. That will help." Sally was back taking accounting classes as part of the prison's education program.

They settled down together in a corner of the lunchroom. The others left them alone; they'd learned it didn't pay to get too close to Sally.

"I also need someone who's good with people," said Mimi.

Not really Sally's forte.

"There's a woman over there. I've been watching her for months." Mimi pointed to a woman in an armchair, surrounded by three other inmates, all hanging on her words. "See how she commands attention? She has people eating out of her hand, doing stuff for her, including some guards. She's an excellent manipulator. We could use someone like that."

Sally watched the woman holding court. "Who is she?"

"She calls herself Dr. Mayberry."

A mother's love. A father's obsession. A son caught in the middle.

Keira's world is shattered when her son's father resurfaces, determined to claim the child he abandoned years ago. As the unwelcome intruder relentlessly pursues his goal, Keira must summon all her strength to protect Daniel from the man who once deserted them both.

Turn the page for a free preview…

MINE: Chapter One

Daniel

It was wrong, all so wrong.

First, they were late. Mom didn't get him up on time. She said she got up early to work on a project, then got so into it she forgot the time. He got that—it happened to him all the time when he was really into something. But gee, Mom. Grown-ups were supposed to have it together. Not getting out of bed at the correct time meant his routine was all messed up, and he had to skip his calming twenty minutes of Lego building time. That was wrong, just wrong.

Then, his red shirt was nowhere to be found. It was Tuesday, so he wore that red shirt. Always. Mom got all in a flap trying to find it. She promised she'd done the laundry and put it away. They finally found the shirt all balled up, trapped between the washing machine and the dryer, still with the grape jelly stain down the front. He didn't care, but Mom said that no, he could not wear it in that condition. So now he had on Thursday's shirt, which would mess things up for later this week.

It was Elizabeth's turn to drive him and his friends to school, but she called to say she was sick. Stuff like that happened, he knew, but still, it threw out their routine. Mom drove them instead. She was an okay driver usually, but this morning she was upset about not waking him up on time, and about the red shirt, so her driving was fast and erratic, not soothing at all. Timothy noticed it and flicked his fingers hard all the way to school, in time with his rocking. Amy didn't seem to care; she chattered the whole way.

Things would be better once he got to the classroom. He liked Ms. Harding; she was a routine kind of person. September had been tough. A lot changed when you moved from grade one to grade two. Not as much of a change as from kindergarten to first grade. Boy, last year was a challenge. But grade two was better. Ms. Harding had routines for *everything*. Once you figured out the patterns, it was comforting to know how things would go.

Daniel froze in the hallway. Behind him, some kid bumped into his back. A shiver went through him, and his fists clenched. Yuck. He hated to be touched unexpectedly.

Something wasn't right. Where was Ms. Harding? She always stood in the doorway to their classroom, giving each student a hug, handshake or high five–their choice. Some kids mixed it up, making a different choice each morning, but not Daniel. He'd made the big decision once and stuck with it. Handshakes were things that people did; he'd studied adults a lot. So that was his choice, something he'd need to get used to all his life.

Hanging back, Daniel watched some of his classmates. At least, he thought they must be his classmates because they entered his classroom. It was sometimes hard to tell because faces often blurred together in a jumble. Unless he spent a lot of time with someone, like his friends, he could get lost in the sea of details and find it hard to recognize individual facial features and match them to a name. He noticed how the kids hesitated in the doorway, looking for Ms. Harding. Then they'd just go into the room and sit down, ignoring that whole hug/handshake/high five routine. It wasn't right and had never happened before.

What a day.

Heels clicked, clicked down the hallway. Mrs. Frey, the principal, approached from the other direction. Noticing Daniel lurking behind the door, she motioned to him to follow her in. "Come on, Daniel. Get in the classroom." She used that impatient tone that Mom got when they were late. Maybe Ms. Frey's mother hadn't woken her up on time, either.

Peeking in the classroom doorway, Daniel blinked. The sunshine through the windows seemed brighter than usual. Maybe someone had washed the panes of glass, removing the dust and grime. Too bad. He preferred it when the light was muted.

The fluorescent lights overhead hummed. Some days, that constant buzz was more annoying than at other times. Today was one of the bad times. Maybe that was why the kids were talking so loudly, to be heard over that incessant buzzing.

Click, click, click, click. Ms. Frey hustled around the room. She stopped to say something to a few of the kids, giving that fake smile adults used when they tried to be polite but had their minds elsewhere and didn't really see you. Geez, her high heels were annoying. Why couldn't she wear soft-soled shoes like Mom and Ms. Harding? Click,

click, click. Maybe if she'd just stand still, it wouldn't be so aggravating.

"Daniel!"

From Mrs. Frey's tone, Daniel guessed that she'd called his name several times already. How was he supposed to hear over all the racket in here?

"Daniel, didn't you hear me? I told you to go put your backpack in your cubby."

Yes. No. No, he hadn't heard her before, but yes, he had now. But no. He didn't want to. The weight felt good on his back, calming him amid the chaos that had replaced his usual classroom.

"Daniel!"

He knew that tone. When Mom used it, it meant he had better get moving.

Dragging the palm of one hand flat against the wall, he shuffled his feet toward the cubicles at the back of the room. Keeping the soles of his feet on the floor helped him feel more grounded, as did his hand following the line of the wall, then the blackboard.

Oops. His fingertips snagged a paper and pulled it off its thumbtack. He stooped to pick it up. The name printed on the top said Randy. Randy wasn't one of his favorite kids. Others seemed to like Randy, but he was too loud for Daniel, too in your face. And, he was fast, rarely staying in one place for long and you never knew what he was going to do next. Probably he wouldn't notice this tear in his picture. Carefully, Daniel replaced it on the bulletin board.

"Daniel. What's taking you so long? We're ready to begin and waiting for you to join us."

Shrugging the straps from his shoulders, Daniel stood with his pack in his hands. His back felt naked without the weight. Slowly, he settled the load on the floor of his cubby.

He kept his head and shoulders inside the space for a minute, relishing the wooden barrier that defined his spot. Plus, his name was neatly printed along the cubicle's top shelf. Daniel. His private spot.

There was that click clicking again, but a bit different this time. Mrs. Frey was no longer strutting around the room, but staying in place, tapping her foot on the floor in front of her. Her hands were on her hips and her eyes looked directly at Daniel. They didn't move off him and her mouth was a straight line. Body language, his mom said. Think about what a person's body language might tell you.

It was so weird that people thought that a *body* could speak, telling you stuff. That's what mouths were for, or at least on most people. He, himself, did not talk much, but had ways to get his meaning across that worked for him. It's not that he *didn't* want to speak, it's just that it was so hard. There were all these words jumbled around in his head, but getting them from his brain onto his tongue was another matter. Sometimes it worked, but mostly it didn't. So why bother trying? He got along okay anyway.

Besides, most people talked too much, so maybe if he didn't, it would all even out.

He tuned into the classroom. Mrs. Frey was standing there with her mouth opening and closing. Sometimes when people spoke, it was like waa, waa, waa in his brain with all the soundings running together, making it hard to distinguish the individual parts. It was especially hard at times like now when there was all this background noise - kids whispering, shifting in their squeaky seats, scratching pencils on paper, the buzzing of the ceiling lights, and...

Startled, he felt something slip across his lap. Almost instantly, everything felt better with the weighted pillow across his thighs. Ms. Lori, the EA, smiled and moved behind him. Placing both hands on his shoulders, she pressed down gently, but firmly. Ms. Lori was the educational assistant in the classroom. She understood. Under the pressure of her hands, his shoulders relaxed.

Within a few minutes, he could make sense of Mrs. Frey's words. His anxiety spiked.

What? Ms. Harding wouldn't be here today? How could that be?

Sick, suddenly sick? That wasn't supposed to happen to teachers.

They had a plan in place, Ms. Harding and his mom. If she was going to be away, she told Mom ahead of time. Then he and Mom went over the social story about what would happen when a substitute teacher came into the room. It was never good, but being prepared made it a bit more tolerable.

But this, this was breaking the rules. There'd been no warning. What was he supposed to do?

There was a light rapping on the door to their classroom.

"Ah, here she is now." Mrs. Frey waved a strange lady into their room. "Class, I'd like you to meet Mrs. Stewart. She'll be your teacher for the day." With one of those smiles that aren't really smiles, Mrs. Frey hurried out the door.

No! No, no, no. This was not right. Ms. Harding was supposed to be here. *She* was their teacher. Daniel rocked back and forth in his seat. His shoulder blades whacked against his seat back. The heels of his sneakers banged the underside of his seat, then burst forward, only to swing back again. The force of his movements increased as he clung to the sides of his chair.

"We'll start with roll call. Raise your hand when I call your name."

No! That was not how it was done. It was Nina's turn to call out the names. It said so right there on the board. This was all going so wrong.

"I guess you must be Daniel, the only one who didn't raise his hand."

He had not heard her say his name. He's not heard her call any of their names after that first one, which was done in so not the right way. Poor Nina. She'd missed her turn. It wasn't fair. The tightening in his chest grew bigger, so big it might suffocate him any minute now.

Crouching, Lori said, "It's okay, Daniel. It'll be all right. Come with me and we'll go get a drink." She moved her hand from his shoulder to his hand. He missed the weight on his shoulder and tilted his head to the side, trying to find that comforting pressure again. That was his focus, not the tug on his hand. His breath came in gasps.

"Ms. Lori, please sit down. You're interrupting our class." The reprimand came from the imposter teacher, pretending to be Ms. Harding. "And you, young man," her steely eyes turned to Daniel. "Stop making that noise and stay still in your seat."

Her gaze was awful, just awful and mean. After one quick peek, Daniel could not bear to meet her eyes.

"And look at me when I'm talking to you." How could she not see that she made this impossible? While it had been just tiny squeaks coming from his mouth before, now they were louder, the sounds strung together in one long chain, building and building.

Ignoring the imposter, Ms. Lori pulled on his fist, tucking her other hand under his upper arm, all but lifting Daniel from his seat.

But it was too late, and all too much.

MINE: Chapter Two

It was recess time. Gathered in the principal's inner sanctum were the principal, Mrs. Frey, substitute teacher Mrs. Stewart, EA Lori Nabuker, and consultant Mel Nichols. It was tight with all four adults huddled around the speakerphone.

"Hello, Ms. Foster. We've had a little problem this morning."

"What? Is Daniel all right? Have you lost him again? I'll be right there."

Mel interrupted. "Hold on, Keira. It's all right. This is Mel Nichols, the consultant. Daniel is right here, and he's fine."

"What's the problem then?"

Mel continued. "The problem was change and there were a lot of changes this morning, enough to throw Daniel off his game."

Keira knew what that likely meant. "What's he doing now?"

"Hey, Keira. It's Lori."

Some of the tension in Keira's shoulders eased. Lori knew Daniel and could read him well. She was a wonderful EA to have in her son's classroom. "What's going on, Lori?" And, if there was a problem, why wasn't Lori with him?

"Ms. Harding's away today." Lori left it at that, knowing Keira would get the significance.

"But I thought we had a plan in place for her absences. I'd work through the social story with Daniel the night before, preparing him for a substitute teacher. I checked my phone and email last night and there was no message from the school." They all knew how surprise changes threw Daniel. It was in everyone's best interests if they prepared him ahead of time for change.

Principal Frey took over. "We had no time to notify you. On her way to school this morning, Ms. Harding was in an accident was taken to hospital to be checked over."

"Is she all right?"

"Bruised and shaken, so she'll be off for a few days, but she'll be fine, she says."

In the silence that followed, Keira's imagination tumbled over itself, envisioning how Daniel might take the shock of his teacher not welcoming him at the door of their classroom. She was almost afraid to ask. "How did things go?"

"Not well." Before anyone else could speak, a stranger's voice spoke. "This is Gloria Stewart. The principal called me in to take Ms. Harding's place today." She cleared her throat. "I've taught for over thirty years, so have experience with students of all ages. Never have I…"

Mel interrupted. "Keira, this is Mel again. As you can imagine, the shock of not seeing his teacher was tough on Daniel. Because all this happened so quickly, there was not time to brief Mrs. Stewart on the plans for the class in general or for Daniel in particular." The things Mel didn't say echoed loudly in the room.

Keira got it. "Was it bad?"

"This is Lori, and yeah, it wasn't good."

"Where is he now? How is he?"

"He's in the sensory room. One of the other EAs is with him, and he's calmer now."

"I'll be right there to get him." Keira began saving the work on her computer.

"No," said Gloria Stewart. "We were just discussing this. I was the teacher in the room at the time of his tantrum. I don't think we should reward this child with a holiday off from school. I agree he needed to calm down, but now that he's quiet, he should return to class, apologize for creating such a ruckus, and do his work like every other child."

"Thank you for your thoughts, Mrs. Stewart," said Principal Frey. "But you've just met this child. Mel, as the autism consultant, what do you suggest?"

"Keira, you know your son, and of course, it's your call." Mel avoided looking at the substitute teacher. "We know him, too, and if you want my opinion, this morning was too much for him. He's more settled now, but he's drained. If you prefer he stay at school, we'll keep things calm for him, but he might be more comfortable at home for the rest of the day. Now that we know Ms. Harding will be away tomorrow as well, we'll have plans in place. We're already working on them, and I'll be teaching in that classroom tomorrow."

"I'll be there in 20 minutes to get my son."

MINE: Chapter Three

At home, Daniel played on the thick Berber carpet, creating action figures with his building blocks. At first glance, he appeared like any other seven-year-old, and most people might think he'd recovered from his morning upset. They might even think that the cranky, old substitute teacher was right, and that Daniel had thrown a fit to get out of doing his schoolwork. As the sub, Gloria Stewart, said during the conference call, what kid wouldn't like to get to go home and play?

Daniel wouldn't, that's who. Keira knew her son. He would not fake a meltdown. He would not purposely do anything to upset his routine, and he knew the regimen to be followed at school.

The tenseness in his neck belied his seemingly unconcerned play. The twitching fingers of his left hand, the way his body started at every squeak of Keira's chair, the way he constantly checked on his mom from the corner of his eye, were all clues that no, Daniel was not all right. He was better than he'd been a few hours ago, but his body was still on high alert.

Thinking of the adrenalin and cortisol that must have run rampant through his small body this morning when he panicked, Keira vowed to do anything to make her child feel safe.

To do that, she needed to stick to their routine, and replicate the environment where Daniel was in his most calm state. That meant getting back to the basics, with just the two of them, in their comfortable, predictable routine. That might mean giving some things up.

Anything. Daniel and his needs came first. She would do anything to protect her son.

That anything included Jake, no matter how much Jake fumed. Oh, he kept his temper in check, but behind his terse words, Keira heard the hurt.

What he asked was nothing unusual. He'd simply called to say he'd be over later and would bring supper, as he did several times a week. Normally, the food and his presence were welcomed by both Keira and Daniel.

Since Jake entered their lives several years ago, they were often now a threesome, rather than the twosome of just Keira and Daniel.

But not tonight.

"I'm sorry, Jake, but it's not a good time."

Silence. "What do you mean?" He spent time with Keira and Daniel more days than not. He'd been there when one of them was sick. On various occasions, he'd held both of them while they puked, washed their faces with a warm cloth, prepared chicken soup. He'd spent hours with Daniel while Keira worked feverishly to meet a contract's deadline. He'd seen them both at their best and at their worst. What did she mean it wasn't a good time? "What's going on, Keira?"

"Daniel had a rough time at school this morning. He needs to be quiet at home for the rest of the day."

Jake looked at the phone. Quiet? Did she think he was a one-man band? He'd spent countless evenings on the couch with Keira and Daniel, watching the endless loops of the videos Daniel so enjoyed. Jake didn't care. Just being there with them, his two favorite people, was enough. "Is he okay?"

"He is now."

"Then what's the problem with me coming over? I planned on bringing his favorite takeout food." Keira could be prickly, but he thought they'd moved past that long ago. "Daniel doesn't mind me. You know that."

It was true. Many times, as the evening wore on, it was Jake's lap Daniel sought, rather than his mom's.

Keira knew Jake and the way his mind worked. Short of hanging up on him, she was going to have to explain. That didn't mean Jake was going to like what he heard. Still, Daniel first... "He had a meltdown at school. I brought him home. When he's been upset like that, we need to go back to the basics, back to the routine he was used to, the one that comforted him."

"Yeah, I get that. I've been around him long enough to know."

True. He got it, at least most times. She did not want to hurt this man, but knew that her next words would do just that. "It needs to be just Daniel and me this evening. He needs to be calm, and know what to expect..."

"What to expect? He expects me to be there. I'm there most evenings, unless I'm working." Jake ran his hands through his hair. "Geez, Keira, I put the kid to bed half the time. He wants me, *me*, to read him his bedtime story." This made no sense. Daniel was used to him, liked him, maybe even loved him, the same way Jake loved this little boy. "Keira, talk to me. Tell me what's going on."

"I'm parenting, Jake. I know what's best for Daniel and best for tonight is just him and me." Her tone changed. "Please understand. I'm just doing what's right for Daniel."

"Yeah? And is this what's right for you, too? For me?"

"Those things don't matter. Only Daniel does and I need to do what I have to do for him."

"How long is my banishment going to last?"

"Jake, don't be like that. Please try to understand."

"How long, Keira?"

"Maybe just for tonight. I need to see how he is tomorrow."

"Fine. Call me tomorrow."

Gently, Keira set her phone back on her desktop. Well, that went about as well as she'd thought it would. A flicker of doubt entered her mind. Was she wrong? Too hard on Jake? After all, Daniel obviously loved the man. The two were close.

Still, this meltdown was a setback. He'd not had one in school at all this year. She needed to get their lives back on an even keel. Consistency and routine were crucial to autistic kids. She'd do what had always worked for them.

Her phone chirped. Jake. He wasn't giving up. At other times, she loved that trait in him, but not this time. She was in mama bear mode and would do what she needed to do for her son.

She glanced at the phone and frowned. Not Jake, but an unknown number. She silenced it.

A self-contained kid, Daniel had always been good at amusing himself. Keira admired that. While other mothers complained they couldn't get a minute to themselves, Keira had the opposite problem. Much of Daniel's toddlerhood had been spent with Keira working to engage him, to have him interact with her.

After his autism diagnosis, things became clearer. She understood why their day did not go well when she put certain clothes on him - clothes with tags or seams that rubbed. They did their shopping first thing in the morning when stores were uncrowded so that he wouldn't get so overwhelmed by the noise and lights and crowds. They frequented the stores that had "quiet shopping hours" where the music was off and the lights less bright.

She learned to go with Daniel's interests and nurture them. Communication was still a challenge, but they'd carved out a good life together, just the two of them.

They'd had to. Everyone else rejected them.

Her phone vibrated. Again. A quick glance ascertained it was not Jake, but an unknown number again. Probably some telemarketer. From across the room, Daniel watched her. Probably wondering why she didn't answer the phone. She silenced it. "Mommy has work to do," she told Daniel.

Did she ever. Grateful that Daniel happily occupied himself, she turned back to her computer monitor. The graphic design contract work she did was ideal for a single mother. She could work around the times when her son needed her. It had been tough in those early years, but she'd gotten the hang of juggling current jobs with the need to pick up new contracts. Working from home suited her and Daniel. Now that he was in school full days, she had more time and her business had picked up, with steady clients recommending her services to new firms. These days, she could even afford to be choosy about which projects she took on.

Her phone vibrated yet another time. Same unknown number. This was getting annoying. Maybe she should turn the phone off, but that went against the grain. For so many years, she'd needed to be available to both clients and the school in case they called her about Daniel. No, she couldn't do it. She silenced the call and shoved the phone to the far corner of her desk.

Like Daniel, Keira could fully focus. It's what let her get so much accomplished, even when she worked in spurts.

Only in a dim part of her consciousness did it register that her pesky phone vibrated with an incoming call. Then it stopped.

Movement out of the corner of her eye snagged her attention. Daniel picked up her phone and held it to his ear.

A male voice came through. "Hello. Hello?"

No, that wasn't Jake's deep timbre.

"Hello, is anyone there? Keira?"

Daniel held the phone out to his mom. Oral communication was not his forte, although he used some words now. This was not one of those times.

Taking the phone from Daniel with a smile of thanks, Keira put the pesky device to her ear. "Hello."

"Keira, is that you? I've been trying to reach you for weeks."

That voice. Something pinged in her memory but didn't make any usable connection. Was it one of her clients? "Who is this, please?"

"It's Mason."

Silence. She only knew one Mason, but that was from long ago. It couldn't be him.

The voice on the phone cleared its throat. "Mason Cooper."

The room around Keira grew smaller. It narrowed to one focal point - Daniel. The child stood staring at her. She pulled him to her side, placing a kiss on the top of his wavy, reddish hair. There were no words for what the name Mason Cooper did to her.

"Yeah, I know. This is a surprise, right?" He waited. "Keira, can you say something?"

"What do you want?"

He laughed.

Once, long ago, Keira had known this man, that laugh, well. This wasn't his humor laugh, it was his nervous one. "Why are you calling me? And how did you get this number?"

"Gotta admit, you weren't easy to find. But a little effort, a little money, and here we are."

"What do you want from me?" Old feelings erupted in her stomach, pushing their way up, getting caught in her throat. Once, he'd taken everything from her, or that's how it had felt at the time.

"My son, of course."

MINE: Chapter Four

That voice. How long since she had last heard it? Wait, she knew exactly how long - Daniel's age, plus six months. Their son's age. No, *her* son's age.

With that voice, the memories tumbled back, over and over each other, the good drowned out by the bad. Those were her darkest days.

College. It had been fun. Moving away from home, taking classes that fit her interests and talents, meeting Mason.

It had been her junior year. The novelty of living in a dormitory had long worn off. Keira was a private person, and the constant presence of others around her was wearying.

When she and Mason started going out together, she spent more and more time at his attic, one-room apartment that was his and his alone. By Christmas of that year, he invited her to move in with him. It only made sense since she was there most of the time, anyway.

Life was good. They got along well and shared the tiny

space with little conflict. Although they didn't talk about permanent commitments, Keira felt like their partnership together was unshakable.

That spring, Mason, who was a year ahead of her, graduated. With his new job came money. Now that he wasn't a poor student, the cramped space irritated him, and he was no longer content to scrimp. Together, they found a better place, bigger, with a kitchen, living room, bedroom, bathroom, and small extra room they called their office. The spaces felt huge compared to the one-room jumble they'd been used to.

It was farther from campus, so Keira had to take two busses, plus walk a bit, but it was worth it to live in such a nice place. Still, with a year of college left to go, Keira's budget was tight. Not a problem, Mason had said. Whereas they used to share in the rent equally, now Mason could pay two-thirds of the cost. That meant that Keira's third taxed her finances, but she picked up more hours at the library where she worked part time. She could handle it for the final eight months of school, then she, too, would have a decent job with more money coming in.

Senior year of college was busy with classes, assignments, as well as working full days on Sunday, and three other 4-hour shifts during the week.

Christmas exams rolled around. Keira's mind was stressed; her body was stressed. But she'd manage, of course she would. Just another five months, then she'd have her degree.

One thing had always been true for Keira - her body followed her mind. When her brain operated in over-drive, her body went out of sync as well. Her menstrual cycle, never perfectly predictable, became irregular when her system became taxed.

When she missed her period in January, the omission didn't register. Final semester. She was busy. She was tired.

When the same thing happened in February, she took note, but thought little of it. This had happened before, lots of times. Plus, she had too much to do, too much she needed to get done to think about anything extraneous.

The flu lingered. It wasn't a violent sort of flu, but one where she felt sick on and off. Food had little appeal, as it didn't stay down well. On the plus side, their toilet bowl was spotless. Since she spent so much time with her head near its rim, she cleaned it at least once a day.

But she was so tired. Just two more months, then school would be over.

Mason, at first supportive of her tummy upsets, grew less patient. "At least go to the doctor, Keira. Get something for it. Barfing several times a week isn't normal, and it stinks up the bathroom."

He was right. It wasn't normal. It signaled an unusual state, one Keira never contemplated happening to her. She was pregnant.

Leaving the doctor's office, she called in sick to work, for the first time ever. She wasn't lying, she truly was nauseous, but now she knew the reason this state plagued her for the last two months. Pregnant. She was going to have a baby, she, and Mason.

Entering the park across the way, Keira found a spot to sit, a place removed from everyone else, a place to contemplate, then savour the news. A baby.

Her initial fear and shock gave way to calm, then a smile. She rested her palm on her still-flat abdomen. A baby. A new life created by the two of them, a new life to cherish and raise together. She smiled to herself, her step lighter as she boarded the bus for home, the nest she and Mason shared.

The smell of bacon frying turned her stomach as Keira opened the door. The popping and sizzling followed behind the aroma of almost burnt toast.

Lovely that Mason was home and had started supper. But bacon? Normally a fan, these last two months changed things. She'd told Mason this, how bacon churned her stomach these days and asked if they could please avoid it. He said it was all in her head. She'd researched to find out why this former fave now sent her gut into revolt. And why bacon? Other meats didn't do it?

But bacon was unique. She'd looked it up at the library. When the fatty acids broke down as it cooked, they turned into compounds of smells and tastes called furans, aldehydes, and ketones. Furans were nutty and sweet, aldehydes grassy, and ketones buttery. Somehow, the combo sent her stomach into rebellion.

She ran to the bathroom to heave.

"You okay, babe?" Mason carefully flipped the bacon strips over so they would cook evenly. A grease bubble popped, and he pulled back his hand, bringing the side of his fist to his mouth, licking the tiny burn spot. "How long is this flu going to last? You need to see a doctor."

Pale, and on the shaky side, Keira emerged from the bathroom and headed to the kitchen sink for a glass of water. "I saw a doctor, and he told me what the problem was."

Mason waited.

"Maybe not exactly a problem, but a reason." Turning to Mason, Keira slid her arms around his waist, a smile of contentment on her face. "Guess what?"

Mason returned her smile and her embrace. "What? Good news, I presume."

She nodded. "Not sure it can get any better than this." Stepping back a half pace so she could see his face, see the joy she knew would be there, she said. "There's a reason my stomach's been so queasy, and I've been tired." Her grin could not get any bigger. "We're pregnant!"

Mason stiffened, his hands frozen in place on Keira's waist. Then his arms fell as he took a pace back. Then two paces, then three. "Say that again."

Her smile slipped a notch. "We're pregnant. The baby will be here in August."

Mason's head shook back and forth. "No." He held up his hands as a barrier between them. "No. This was not part of the plan. No way."

"I know we hadn't planned it, hadn't talked about it, but it happened anyway." Far less sure of herself now, "Aren't you pleased?"

Mason continued to shake his head from side to side as his feet put more distance between himself and Keira. Now he began to pace, striding the length of the living room and back again. Hands fisted on either side of his head. As if talking more to himself than to his girlfriend, he muttered as he paced. "No. No way. I'm not having a kid. I *can't* have a kid. A kid would ruin everything." His strides grew faster and longer.

He stopped directly in front of Keira, his nose just inches from hers. "You're getting rid of it, right?"

Keira's eyes widened, and she stepped back. Who was this man? "No, of course not. I'm past 12 weeks, so it's too late, anyway, even if I wanted to, which I don't." Life was sacred. Hadn't she learned that lesson all her life?

"I'm outa here, then. I want no part of this." Snatching up his jacket, Mason left, the door slamming after him.

MINE: Chapter Five

"Your son? *Your* son?" Keira stared at the phone in her hand, then at the seven-year-old playing on the carpet. How dare Mason, the man who had deserted and rejected them, call Daniel his son?

Glancing at the child, she consciously lowered her voice. Daniel was sensitive to moods, and she didn't want him any more upset than he had been earlier that day. Giving her son a smile and a one-armed hug, she left the room. Think. Where best to go? With Daniel's acute hearing, she didn't want him listening to even this one-sided conversation.

Upstairs in the bathroom, she turned on the faucet and sat on the side of the tub. The noise of the running water should mask her words in case Daniel came by to listen. "Okay. What is this all about, Mason, and make it quick. I'm busy."

"What, no how are you, long time no see and how's your life been and all that?"

Controlling her breathing, Keira unclenched her jaw before replying. "I don't care how your life's been. After the way you ran out on us, I never want to hear of you or your existence again. Goodbye and good riddance."

Too bad she didn't have one of those old, corded phones from the 80s, one that she could actually slam back onto a receiver. Somehow, pushing the red disconnect button on a smart phone didn't have the same panache.

Keira realized she was trembling. And cold, oh so cold. She tried to beat back the images from the darkest time of her life, but they persisted, breaking through the barricades she'd fought so hard to erect.

She turned off the faucet, but the running water gave her an idea. Leaving the bathroom, she checked on Daniel, telling him she was going to take a bath. She pressed play on his favorite video. Yeah, she knew that television was a terrible babysitter, but when needs must... He'd be content for at least 45 minutes, maybe more if he watched it over again.

After ensuring that the front and back door were locked, she returned her phone to the charger on her desk and gathered her comfiest flannel pajamas. She hesitated. Oil or bubble bath? She added a generous dollop of lilac-scented oil, then two, but bubbles would be good, too. Scanning the bottles lined up on the side of the tub, she chose lavender bubble bath. Lilac and lavender - both L words, both flowers, both *purple* flowers. How could they not work well together? She dumped in several dollops, waited a few moments, then added more. Why not? She needed all the comfort she could get while she allowed her thoughts to stray to Mason and the worst year of her life.

Disrobing, Keira gathered her hair into a loose knot on top of her head, then sank into the warm, silky, fragrant water.

Only then did she let the tears come.

Rarely did Keira feel sorry for herself. Holding a pity party was not her style. She should know - she'd tried it and it hadn't helped, not one whit.

Visions of the night Mason fled rolled over her.

When he had left, slamming the door, Keira ran after him. He heard her, she knew he did, yet his stride didn't slow. He almost ran to his motorcycle, hopped on, and sped away, without one glance back at the woman who held him in the center of her world.

Back in their suite, Keira shut, but didn't lock the door. Somehow, with it unlocked, it seemed more inviting for Mason's return. And she knew he would return. Of course he would. He was just shocked.

Well, she'd been shocked herself when the doctor told her the results of the pregnancy test. Shocked, because the possibility never occurred to her, and she'd not given much thought to having kids. Maybe one day, in that hazy future, but her life and babies were not strands she'd thought of weaving together.

But as she left the medical clinic with a prescription for prenatal vitamins in her hand, a small smile came to her lips. Then a bigger one.

No, it wasn't planned, but not everything in life was. She'd be finished her degree before the baby was born. Mason had a good job, they had a nice place to live with plenty of room for an infant, and within the next year Keira would start her career as well.

The nurse practitioner talked about baby hormones. She explained that the fatigue Keira experienced was normal, and many pregnant women felt they were more emotional than usual.

That was it. That was the reason Keira sank to the floor by the unlocked door and sobbed.

It was probably her fault. She had not broken the news to Mason very well. She should have warmed up to the announcement. She should have reassured him it was going to be all right, that she could handle this, that *they* could handle it. Surely, he'd come to love the idea as much as she did already.

A draft on her back woke Keira. She stretched, trying to ease into a more comfortable position. The crack under the door let in a cool breeze. How had she never noticed that before?

It was dark in the apartment. When she'd cried herself into an exhausted sleep, it had been light out. Now it was night. Had Mason returned without waking her?

"Mason," she called.

Nothing.

Using the doorknob for leverage, Keira hoisted herself to her feet, reaching for the light switch. She blinked as light flooded the kitchen and entryway. "Mason," she called again. She checked the living room, the bedroom, the study, and the bathroom. No, she was alone. Where was Mason? He rarely stayed out this late, and not without letting her know where he'd be.

Her phone. Of course. She must have slept right through it, ringing or the chime of a text message. Messages. There were likely several of them, since it was almost six hours ago that Mason had left.

Digging through her purse, she pulled out her phone. Nothing. Yes, it was charged, but there was not one text from Mason, and no missed calls.

Poor guy. He must be really upset. How could she have just blurted out the news like that? She prepared a sandwich for him, covered it in plastic wrap, and set it in the fridge. She put a note on the table, letting him know to look for the sandwich. Then she washed her face and headed to bed.

The next morning, she'd woken up alone. A search of the apartment showed no evidence that Mason had returned. Shaken and hungry from skipping supper the day before, Keira gulped down some milk and a banana, then tried to repair the ravages hours of crying had left on her face.

No matter how she felt or looked, she had to go to class. It was the final semester of her final year, not the time to slack off. Brushing her hands over her midsection, Keira realized that now, more than ever, it was crucial to finish her schooling.

It was late afternoon before Keira returned to their apartment. As she unlocked the door, she called, "Mason." Then she listened to the silence. She comforted herself knowing that it would be unusual for Mason to be home from work this early. She busied herself with browning meat and preparing supper. Tonight, they'd have a good meal, then sit down and really talk about this. They'd snuggle on the couch and plan. It would be good.

Six o'clock came. Seven o'clock, then nine. Still no Mason. She'd called his cell phone countless times, but her calls went to voicemail, her texts unanswered. Something must have come up at work.

Finally, she wrapped up their dinner, stowing the uneaten food in the fridge. Stifling a yawn, she went into their bedroom. A shower would help. Or maybe a bath.

Opening a dresser drawer, she reached in for a fresh nightgown, noticing something odd. Mason's drawer was not fully shut. Really odd. Mason had a thing about that. It irked him when drawers or cupboards were not fully closed. A quirk of his, for sure, but one she could live with. But why was *his* drawer slightly open? *She* might make that mistake, but not Mason. As she went to shut it for him, she could see the wooden bottom to the drawer. That drawer was full of his socks and underwear. Why did she not see the usual jumble?

Yanking it open, she saw it was empty. What? She pulled open the other drawers he used. All empty. Rushing to the closet, her eyes took in the barren left side of the closet rod. Gone. What happened to Mason's clothes?

Next, she checked the bathroom. Gone. All of Mason's toiletries were missing.

With dread filling her bones to the marrow, her feet dragged their way into the study that they shared. Pulling open the closet door, she saw that Mason's suitcases were no longer stacked in the corner. Whirling, her eyes scanned the desk. His laptop wasn't there; neither was his printer nor any of the things he cluttered their shared space with. Gone. All of it. Just like Mason.

Grab your copy...
vinci-books.com/MINE